The
Lost Treasure of
Captain Kidd

The Lost Treasure of Captain Kidd

PETER LOURIE

BOYDS MILLS PRESS

For my son
Walker

A special thanks to Captain John Cutten. If it were not for his adventurous spirit and enthusiasm for Hudson pirates, this book would never have been born.

Text copyright ©1996 by Peter Lourie

Published by Caroline House
Boyds Mills Press, Inc.
A Highlights Company
815 Church Street
Honesdale, Pennsylvania 18431
Printed in the United States of America

Publisher Cataloging-in-Publication Data
Lourie, Peter
        The Lost Treasure of Captain Kidd / by Peter Lourie.—1st ed.
[96]p. :ill. ; cm.
Summary: Two boys living along the Hudson River track historical clues and try to elude a crazed treasure-hunter as they search for bounty rumored to have been hidden in 1699.
ISBN 1-56397-851-2
[1.Kidd, William, d.1701. 2. Buried treasure—Fiction. 3. Hudson River Valley (N.Y. and N.J.)—Fiction 4. Adventure and adventurers—Fiction
813.54 [F]—dc20 1996 AC CIP
Library of Congress Catalog Card Number 99-63671

First edition, 2000
The text of this book is set in 12-point Berkeley Book.

10 9 8 7 6 5 4 3

CONTENTS

The Hudson Highlands

Hudson River

Bannerman's Island

N
W   E
S

Storm King Mountain

Indian Brook

West Point

Garrison

Peekskill

Dunderberg Mountain

Troy
Albany

Catskill   Hudson

Kingston   Rhinebeck
Poughkeepsie
Newburgh   Beacon
West Point   Peeksill

New York

CHAPTER 1

PARTNERS

KILLIAN AND I WERE SITTING ON THE TOWN DOCK after school picturing what it would be like to find Captain Kidd's buried treasure.

"I'll tell you what's going to happen," Killian said.

"No. Let *me* begin."

"Okay, go ahead. I don't care because I know what's going to happen when I find the treasure." Killian sat with his pants rolled up, dipping his toes into the lapping waves of the Hudson.

"*It's dusk,*" I said, but not in my usual voice.

"Just say it normal, Alex."

"I'm trying." But it came out in my storytelling voice.

"*It's dusk and the river's flat like a mirror. The moon rises over the Highlands. We take turns with the shovel, digging a big pit. We dig late into the night. Our backs ache. Suddenly, the shovel hits something—not rock, but metal! CHINK.*"

"Chink chink chink." Killian laughed, his smile a little crazy today, his sea-blue eyes glistening with enthusiasm.

"Let *me* finish, Kill. Will ya?"

"All right, all right, go ahead. But you got to finish it."

"We hardly notice the wind picking up from the south while we work. The river grows rough, the moon lighting the crest of the waves."

Again Killian butted in. "The south wind carries a smell of tropical flowers."

"I'm telling the story. *Stop* interrupting me, will ya?"

"Okay, okay." Killian's smile hung on his face like a hurricane lantern. He looked so impatient.

"We dive into the pit and start scooping the earth away like archaeologists in fast motion. In a few hours we dig that old treasure chest free of the dirt, but it's too heavy to budge. We have to work fast."

"A storm's coming in."

"Yeah, maybe even a tornado. *We're kneeling in the bottom of the pit. I lift the metal lid of the chest with two hands while you prop it open with a branch or something. Together we reach inside the ancient darkness, into Captain Kidd's secret. . . and. . ."*

"Yeah, go on. Finish it." Killian glared at me, his smile gone.

"I can't."

Killian knew I had a hard time ending the story. My imagination got fuzzy, like static on the television. Maybe the treasure doesn't exist, I thought. Maybe two kids couldn't find something lost for nearly three hundred years.

Killian had no such doubt. He was convinced he would find gold. Killian grew up hearing the Captain Kidd story. He'd come to believe it the way you believe in God after years of Sunday school.

"Now let *me* finish," he snapped. "*I* reach into the chest. *I* grab a fistful of *doubloons!*"

He said "doubloons" as if there were five Os in the last syllable—doublooooons.

"That's all there is to it. I don't know what your problem is, Alex." Killian shook his head, disgusted.

Killian knew the river and its stories better than most adults did. Every April, from the time he was five years old, Killian had helped his dad, a Hudson River fisherman, and his uncle haul shad nets. During long hours of fishing, the men told stories about pirates on the Hudson. The notorious William Kidd had sailed upriver with a treasure, but no one knew where he buried it. Killian swore he would be the first to find the gold.

Last year Killian's father had quit fishing altogether. There was more money working road construction, he said. The Hudson fishing industry had died with the pollution getting so bad. Only the shad were left, and the season was too short to be worth the effort.

"Stop staring at me, Killian."

"I'm not staring. I just can't understand why you keep forgetting the story. Like I told you, the pirate was heading upriver to see his friend in Albany. He had gold aboard. His ship went down in a storm. He was coming from the Caribbean. Do you know what the Caribbean is, Alex?"

"No."

"For cripe's sake. How many times have I told you! That's *doubloon* country!"

"Aw, you and your doubloons. What's a doubloon anyway? Why couldn't it be emeralds or rubies or diamonds or Incan sun disks or silk or pearls? The treasure could be anything."

"NO, NO, NO it can't!" Killian shouted. He stood up, turned, and stomped off, his shoes in his hands.

"Maybe I'm going to cut you out of this whole thing!" he yelled back at me.

"Come on, Killian. Okay, it's doubloons. Whatever you want. I don't care."

Calling out after him never did any good when Killian got into one of his moods. Sometimes when he stormed off like this, he'd walk for hours through the Highlands. Or else he'd take his dad's twelve-foot Alumacraft with an outboard motor and head out to some island to sit alone and dream of doubloons.

I don't know why he was so fixed on doubloons. Maybe it was the dream he kept having. In his pirate dream, thousands of gold coins were scattered along shore, glowing in the moonlight.

Most kids in school were afraid of Killian. He was fourteen, almost a year older than everyone else, and he was big. He had done some crazy things, like jumping out of a second-floor window to turn somersaults before landing on his feet on the playground. He had taken ropes and rappeled off the town smokestack at midnight. Kids left him pretty much alone.

Sure, Killian had a reckless streak, but in school he was quiet to an extreme. Maybe his silence made kids feel uneasy. Maybe they thought Killian didn't like them. Fact is, Killian didn't care what anybody else was thinking.

I wasn't scared of Killian. We hit it off from the beginning. The river brought us together, and the lure of treasure hunting. There's some kind of spell surrounding a treasure, and we were caught up in it from the very first day we met.

Our friendship had begun last September when my mom and dad moved us from New York City up the Hudson to the village of Cold Spring. After the first day of school I strolled over to the town dock, not far from our new house. Killian was skipping rocks on the glassy river. No wind. No waves. Just a hot glare.

"You new in town?" he finally said, after I'd been there for quite a while.

"Yeah."

Killian kept his eyes on the flat stones as they zipped and hopped three, five, even seven times before sinking out of sight.

"Know anything about rivers?"

"Nope. You ever go out there?"

Killian laughed. "Guess I should. My dad's a fisherman."

Right away I asked if he would take me out someday. It looked so peaceful.

"Don't let that calm water trick you. The Hudson can be rough—and deadly. On a calm day like this, a big wind can swoop outta nowhere."

Killian looked at me hard for a moment and then went back to skipping rocks. Suddenly, out of the blue, he asked, "Want to be a partner?"

"Sure," I said. "What do I have to do?"

"Nothing much. Just a little treasure hunting. That's all."

"A little?" I asked.

"Okay, big," he said.

"What kind of treasure?"

"Pirate treasure. Doubloons," he said. "When I find it, I'm gonna quit school, buy a fishing boat, and go to sea."

He picked up another skipping rock and snapped it across the watery mirror.

"What would *you* do if you found it?"

Killian was testing me. Seeing if I was serious about helping him find Kidd's loot.

"I'd give some to my dad," I said.

Killian checked his next throw and turned to face me.

"Your *dad*? What does *he* need it for?"

Killian's stare was not friendly.

"My dad's having money trouble, that's all. I'd like to help him if I can." Now I felt stupid for being honest. I should have made something up. So I said, "But I'd only give him a little. How much would I get, anyway?"

With a vengeance, Killian snapped a flat rock as big as his hand over the water. It skipped only one jump before plopping out of sight.

"Fifty-fifty split," Killian said. "And you'll learn about the river, too."

Over his shoulder, he mused, "You know, I think I love this old river more than any human being."

"More than your dad or mom?" I asked.

He nodded yes.

In the eight months that we had been friends we'd had only a few serious arguments. Mostly we got along great. But when he stormed off so angry about the doubloons that day, I decided to bike down to where he lived in Garrison, across from West Point. The Maguires' house was perched on a rock ledge 157 steps above his dad's dock. When the light was almost gone from the sky, I heard the buzz of the Alumacraft returning. It was rounding Constitution Island from the north.

A moving dot in wild spray at first, the dot got bigger until Killian cut the motor a few feet before he might have crashed into the dock. The boat's wake washed over and drenched me.

"Real funny," I said. There was a side of Killian I still didn't understand. Sometimes he acted plain mean.

He tied the boat to the cleats on the dock and sat down. Surprisingly, his foul mood had vanished. He seemed unusually calm.

"What'd you find out? Something important?"

"Don't worry, Alex." Killian's smile was hardly visible in the dwindling light. "Our search is over."

"*Over*? What do you mean? We haven't even *begun* to search for the treasure."

"In a few weeks we're gonna take that sucker outta there. You'll see."

"But how do you know?"

Killian drew up close to me, his smile now as big as the moon.

He whispered, "Because, Alex—*I just found a real treasure hunter, and he's gonna lead us right to it.*"

CHAPTER 2

A DOG'S GHOST

THE NEXT DAY, AFTER SCHOOL, Killian came back to meet me at the town dock in the Alumacraft.

"Come on. Hop in," he said. "You gotta meet this guy."

Killian pulled the starting cord. The motor roared and smoked like ten cherry bombs. He shifted into forward gear, and we sped out from the Cold Spring dock into moderate chop at ten miles an hour heading north. Killian's hair flew all over his face in the wind as we passed Storm King and Breakneck Mountain.

The big chunks of river ice had disappeared from the Hudson in early April, but the water was still chilly. In another few weeks, when school let out, we planned to explore the river in the Alumacraft every day. Killian promised he'd teach me how to run it myself.

I could see we were heading straight for Bannerman's Island. At the top of the Hudson Highlands, Bannerman's was a mysterious place I had seen from the train. The little island was dominated by a strange wreck of a castle.

"The island's haunted, you know," Killian said. "Indians never made camp here. They thought it was cursed."

As we drew closer, the crumbling seven-story replica of a Scottish castle sure seemed spooky.

"Who built this place, anyway?"

Killian dragged the boat a few feet up the beach, directly below a deteriorating hundred-foot-high brick wall. At the top we could see the words carved in brick:

BANNERMAN'S ISLAND ARSENAL

Killian said, "Old Man Bannerman built this in 1900. A warehouse. He stored guns and saddles and military stuff here. He sold them to foreign countries. When he died, the place caved in. I know kids who found old guns and bayonets in the bushes."

Fires had gutted all seven stories. One explosion in the ammunition room had shot half a turret into the river, Killian said. Lucky no ship was passing by.

Killian led the way through brambles, through falling-down passageways, over broken brick, around the flimsy castle walls, and up the hill in back. In a crumbling doorway I glimpsed weeds growing out of the rubble, and stunted trees.

"I wouldn't want to spend the night in this place."

Killian said, "Someday we could."

I smelled woodsmoke before I saw the man. A little cave set back into rock hid the chair on which he was sitting. Perhaps forty years old, the man had black wild hair, a long black beard, thick eyebrows all tangled up. He wore a coat with rips along the sleeves. He smelled of woodsmoke and fish. Eyeglasses perched on his nose with a string around his neck made him look like a crazy librarian.

When he spoke, his voice was mean and sharp.

"So it's you again, kid. Back already? Brought a friend, eh?"

When the glasses fell to his chest, he was like nobody I'd ever met in a library. His eyes was to melt into his skull, bleary grey and desperate.

Killian, fearless, said, "This is my partner, Alex. Tell him what you told me about the treasure, would you, Mr. Cruger?"

Cruger sneered. "Two visits in two days, and I ain't seen nobody for months 'til you come along, kid. Why should I tell you anything?"

"Maybe we should leave, Kill," I said.

"Your partner's right. Maybe you should go, before you get into this too deep."

Cruger coughed and laughed at the same time, his laugh like the bark of a sick dog. Right away I didn't trust him.

"But, hey, I was young once," he said. His smile was big and fake. "This is kids' stuff, right, so why run? You come this far, ain't you? You want to hear about Kidd's gold or not?"

"Sure," said Killian. "Tell Alex what you told me."

Fishing tackle—line, hooks, floats, and nets—hung from the wall of the shelter on nails hammered into the rock. Sooty pots and pans were scattered everywhere. Fish bones littered the packed dirt of the cave floor. Two big nets were heaped on the ground near the fire.

I noticed some topographic maps in one corner of the cave. Four or five maps were stuck to the wall with black marks on them. Hundreds of other maps had been stacked neatly in rows on the floor of the cave.

"Sit down, kids. Or should I say, my little treasure hunters? Ha!"

We sat on old fish bones, brittle as glass.

Abruptly Cruger stood up.

"I'll tell you what I know, what any fisherman knows on the river, and then you can go and try your luck, and never come back. This here's *my* island." Cruger sneezed. He wiped his mouth on his sleeve. "I met your dad once, kid. He's a fisherman, ain't he?"

"Yes," Killian said. "But he works the roads, too. Fishing's no good."

Killian nodded at Cruger's fish tackle. "I guess you know about the fishing?"

"Yep. The river ain't like them old days . . ." Cruger made a sharp noise in his throat while his grey eyes wandered off to the sky. Then he turned. He stared with a kind of hateful look first at Killian, then at me.

"Listen, you can believe this or not. I don't care. Some's gonna think you crazy. There's a legend in these Highlands. Folks say the pirate Captain William Kidd himself was sailing up here in 1699 when a storm blew his ship into the rocks. Before it sank, he rowed his treasure ashore. He lugged it up a mountain to bury it. He found a big tree to mark the spot. But before he buried it, he sliced the throat of his dog. Like this."

Cruger drew a forefinger across his neck and laughed one of the craziest bandito laughs I ever heard.

"Scare you boys?" Cruger leered. "No? Well, it should. Because this wasn't no ordinary dog. It was a 200-pound mastiff, *a guard dog*. Kidd buried the dog's body over the treasure because he knew that anyone—ANYONE—who ever went looking for his gold would be haunted by the ghost of the dog that would rise up out of the grave and never—NEVER—leave the treasure hunter alone."

Cruger spat out the Kidd legend in rapid fire like you'd spit out a bad taste in your mouth. But it was clear he knew the story by heart.

Near the fire I spotted a book. On its side was printed "Clermont Library." I tapped Killian's knee and pointed to the book.

Killian said, "You ever go looking for the treasure, mister?"

Cruger took a rapid step forward, then he lunged for his chair. Everything he did was jerky and strange.

"That's all I know, kid. There ain't no treasure on *this* island, I can tell you that. Now get outta here. I don't want boys sneakin' round my island. Besides . . ." His leer had turned to a scowl. "There ain't no such thing as treasure anyway! Ha ha ha." His laugh was creepy. "Everyone knows that. Now git."

Hiking back down through the brambles, we heard him shout, "I guess I won't be seeing you fellows again. 'Cause if I do . . ."

Cruger's laugh was lost in the wind.

CHAPTER 3

A Clue

KILLIAN SHUT DOWN THE MOTOR so we could drift over World's End, the deepest part of the Hudson. Over his thin face had settled a contented look, like the smile of a fanatic handing out pamphlets on street corners.

"What are you so happy about?"

"It's two hundred feet deep here, you know."

"So?"

The boat bounced in the chop. I kept an eye out for barges. Killian once had told me that a tug pulling a barge in maximum ebb tide could go fifteen knots, or about twenty miles per hour. Tugs with barges can't stop or turn quick enough for little boats like ours. We would have to get out of the way fast or we'd get plowed under.

"So what do you make of that guy, Kill? And that story about the dog's ghost?"

"He's full of baloney about one thing."

"What's that?"

"If he's a fisherman, then where's his fishing boat?"

"Hey, yeah. We didn't see any boat. How does he get to the mainland, anyway? Swim?"

"Doubt it."

"He's looking for the treasure, isn't he, Kill?"

"I'm sure of it."

"Then why did he tell us anything?"

"He's trying to get us on the wrong track. And he's trying to scare us off. I say we stick close to him. He'll take us right where we want to go. First thing, though, I'm going back to Bannerman's Island to find out more. Want to explore it with me?"

"Are you kidding? He'll see us!"

Killian was glaring at me again. "What's the matter? Afraid?"

"I am *not* afraid."

"We'll go at night then."

"Nighttime? But I'll have to sneak out."

"So sneak out, what do I care!"

"Okay, I'll go with you," I said hastily. "Do you think that book was some kind of clue, Kill?"

"Well, you remember Clermont, don't you? That's Livingston's old estate."

"Livingston?"

"Don't you remember anything??? He's the guy who hired Kidd to become a pirate."

"Yeah, yeah, I know, I know." I remembered the name Clermont, but I was fuzzy on exactly who Livingston was.

Killian shook his head, looking as if he might stomp off in one of his fits again. Problem was, there was nowhere to stomp. He'd have to swim.

I felt better when his voice grew softer. I could see he was trying to be patient.

"Listen, Alex, you're never going to find anything unless you know history, for cripe's sake. History is everything."

Killian pulled the starting cord and we were off like a shot. We hadn't gone a hundred yards when he shouted over the buzz and the wind, "Cruuuger's lyyying. He's after the gooold! But I'm gonna beat him to it! I'm *gonna crack this nut.*" Killian whooped.

That weird grin was back on his face, determined, smug. He cut the motor one more time.

A red tug dragging an empty oil barge high out of the water had just cleared the ninety-degreee turn around Constitution Island and was picking up speed and heading straight for us.

"What the heck are you doing?" Surely Killian could see the barge.

"Relax, will you? We got time yet," said Killian as he leaned back against the outboard motor and put his feet up on the seat between us.

His smile was now the same smile of defiance I had seen last fall when another kid bet Killian five dollars he couldn't jump out of Mrs. Dobson's second-story window and land on his feet. Killian, grinning serenely, had said, "You're on," and they shook hands. He took a wild run at the open window, leaping way out, doing a full somersault before landing like a cat on the playground. All of us were cheering and calling him from the window, but Killian didn't even look up. He simply turned and walked home. He didn't even collect his money.

"Killian, are you *crazy?* We better get out of here." I could hear the deep drone of the tug engines bearing down on us.

Killian reached into his shirt. He pulled out a small thick piece of paper and unfolded it on the floor of the Alumacraft, out of the wind.

"See those marks?"

"Oh my God. Killian! You *stole* that. That's one of Cruger's maps!"

"Those marks must be treasure locations. Look. See the dates beside each place? And here's some writing . . ."

"You ripped it right off the wall? He's gonna *kill* us."

Killian studied the map, his head bent low, not noticing the progress of the tug.

"Killian, please please please, let's get the heck out of here."

"Wanna take the helm?"

"Move over."

The tug was now blowing its fog horn. BOOOP BOOOOOP.

I could see the captain in the pilot house furiously waving at us. I traded places with Killian. I pulled the starting cord. Nothing happened. I pulled and pulled and pulled.

"Try the choke."

"What choke?" BOOOOOOOOOOOP.

"Here. This little button here." Killian pulled out a little button. Again I tugged the cord with all my strength. The motor fired up in forward gear and we both fell over the seats. The motor smoked and died. Still Killian did not look nervous. He jammed the choke in and pulled the cord a hard one.

"You have to start in neutral, Alex. You'll get the hang of it."

He threw the gears into forward. I grabbed and twisted the handle and we were off in the wind. Killian clutched the map close to his chest. He sniffed the spring air with a carefree delight that was positively spooky in the face of danger. He didn't care that the tug was so close we could hear the captain cursing at us through a megaphone.

Killian didn't care about anything except treasure.

He didn't even care that his boat was in the hands of a novice, or that we nearly flipped when the four-foot waves from the tug hit us broadside. Killian was definitely in another world, a world where even stealing didn't bother him. For the first time since we met, I wondered who Killiam Maguire really was. And I realized that one—or both—of us could get killed trying to find the treasure of Captain Kidd.

CHAPTER 4

KILLIAN

ALL THROUGH MAY, Killian was getting more reckless, more moody. He was taking more risks. It scared me. But a real treasure hunter *has* to take risks, I kept telling myself.

Killian had the makings of a serious treasure hunter, all right. He often told me about his dream. He said he was beginning to feel "close to Captain Kidd," whatever that meant.

Even before we met Cruger, in late April and early May when the yellow forsythia bloomed along the riverbank, Killian had taken two whole weeks off from school to fish for shad with his Uncle George. His father refused to go. "The river's dead," Killian's father told him. "There ain't no turning 'round in life, son. Sometimes you just gotta move forward and never look back."

Killian had told me one day, "I hate my dad."

Quickly I said, "You don't really *hate* him."

"Yes I do," he said, his face in a scowl. "Not only did he give up fishing and the river, now he and Mom are thinking about selling the house and moving to Florida. I hate Florida, too."

Killian said he would never go with them. He would run away first.

Fishing with his uncle had made Killian happy for a while, although I saw him only briefly during those two weeks. The shad ran by the thousands, he said, which must have made it even harder that his dad wasn't with them.

Killian and his uncle worked the flood tide, which runs every six hours and brings the spawning shad inland from the sea. They fished the Kingston flats and off the west shore of Bannerman's Island, where shad fishermen had worked for as long as anyone could remember.

Later, he told me, "Alex, you can't imagine how hard a fisherman works. There's nothing to compare it to. You fish all day. All night with the tides. Sometimes the cold spray, the driving spring rain, the winds feel more like winter. Such long hours of hauling. Digging up a treasure would be easy compared to hauling nets."

One night on the Hudson it had even snowed, Killian thought, but he couldn't be sure because lack of sleep made him see things out there on the river that might not be real. It might have been pollen, not snow at all.

When Killian had come back to class in mid-May, he looked exhausted. Something had changed in him. Everyone noticed the difference. The teachers began to keep him after school for not paying attention to the lessons. They probably thought it was just spring fever, but I knew different. All through the school day Killian's eyes would stray from the classroom, those sea-blue eyes gazing intently out the window at the water, fixed on the great river distance, on the hard, brown flatness of the quiet days or the wild spume of the blowing whitecaps. Below the school, the Hudson was always changing. It was like a fascinating book to Killian, which he read compulsively.

What had changed him, I think, were two things—a wisp of

smoke on Bannerman's Island and his recurring pirate dream, fast becoming a nightmare.

Fishing the flood tide, Killian's Uncle George had spotted smoke coming from the island. The smoke curled above the towers of the decrepit arsenal. Someone must be camping there. It sure was an odd sight, the fisherman had said, very odd indeed. In fact, he'd never seen any smoke on the island before.

The idea of someone actually living on that weird, dead island intrigued Killian. He wondered what kind of person would live there permanently. That's when Killian had vowed to explore the island.

The other thing that haunted Killian was the dream itself. I never realized that dreams could change your personality. But Killian talked to me about his pirate dream every day.

"It's so real," he would say, sitting on the dock by the water. "Alex, I can see a thousand doubloons scattered along the Hudson shoreline, glowing in moonlight. The buccaneer himself is standing in the moon shadow of a big tree. It's just as clear as I can see *you*, Alex.

"Captain Kidd—he's ten feet tall. He's got a big hat on, and a bandanna over his forehead. His shirt is burlap, his pantaloons stained with blood," Killian said. "I see daggers in his belt. He's got hoops of silver in his ears. I swear.

"And his arm is outstretched. His long, ghostly arm is raised. I think it's a sign of peace. Kidd's finger is pointing at me, to come closer. He wants me to see the secret burying of the gold. I know it, Alex. I just know it."

In fact, the dream was so real to Killian that one day in June, under a perfect blue sky, as we were trying with little luck to skip rocks over a choppy river, he said to me, "Life's a dream, Alex. And dreams are the reality."

Talk like that scared me. The big tree scared me—Killian's dream about the tree and Cruger's story about the dog under the tree were beginning to match up. Yes, I was scared, but I took this as a sign, too, that we were getting close to the treasure. No matter how strange Killian might seem to everyone else, he was my partner and I would never desert him. Especially not when we were about to start digging.

But where? Soon we had to find a place to dig.

CHAPTER 5

JUNK

"**C**AN I DEPEND ON YOU?" Killian had to shout through the din of the school cafeteria. He looked at me doubtfully.

"I got the canoe," he said. "You're not going to bug out on me, are you? All set for tonight?"

"Yeah, sure," I said. "But I have to be home by four-thirty. That's when my dad gets up."

My father always set the coffee machine as an alarm in the morning, then showered and stumbled down the hill to catch the 5:20 train to Manhattan, long before daylight reached the Highlands. "We're just like cattle being herded," he was fond of saying. He hated the crowded commute—mostly, I think, because he *had* to commute.

One day last year, when we still lived in New York City, he had said, "Let's get out of this bloody rat race." That Sunday we drove north looking for a town to live in. Mom, Dad, and I all knew we weren't moving for any reason except that Dad had lost his job, and we were running out of money.

"Cold Spring-on-Hudson seems like a perfect village for a *poor* family," Mom said as we drove down Main Street's alleyway of antique shops. I saw Dad squint and grind his teeth when she said it so meanly. Again they started arguing over money, and I closed my ears. When I first spotted the wide river at the bottom of Main Street with the mountains behind it, I ran to the dock. It was beautiful.

We rented a tiny house on Fish Market Street in Cold Spring and moved up for the beginning of the school year. Now Dad complained constantly about his hour-and-a-half commute to the city and his new job. "That's three bloody hours on a cattle car! I never even see my own family. I leave in the dark and return in the dark. Might as well work the graveyard shift and sleep all day."

Mom didn't seem happy these days, either. She was forever reminding Dad and me that we couldn't afford this item or that "luxury," as she called anything that wasn't "essential to living and breathing."

"If you don't like the commute so much, dear," she'd say, "try a little harder for some more money and we'll move back down." She knew how to get him bull-charging angry. I guess it was because she herself wasn't happy, but she didn't have to pick on him so much.

Around February last year, in the endless days of heavy wet snow and sleet and grey skies over the brooding Highlands, Dad was sitting in his big armchair reading. His frown was hidden behind the Sunday *New York Times*. I told him I was going out to play and I shut the front door, but I doubled back and stood in the hall. I peeked around the corner. Dad had put the newspaper down on his lap. He grabbed his head in both hands and shook it side to side like a coconut. I'd never seen him act like that. He looked like he had a terrible headache.

I was about to run over and help when I heard his voice all

raspy and strange. It didn't sound like my father at all. He said over and over, as if making a desperate prayer, "Oh God, please give me a million dollars, please, please."

At that very instant I knew I had to find Killian's treasure even if I didn't really believe it existed. Dad was in some kind of deep money trouble. If I didn't find the treasure, for all I knew, something awful might happen to him, or to us as a family.

It was past midnight. Killian pulled the canoe from the bushes. I don't know how he found it because a thick river fog had covered everything. The river was waveless, the tide slack, neither ebbing nor flooding.

"You hold the flashlight, Alex."

Killian lifted the small aluminum canoe over the boulders that formed the bed of the railroad track and slid it quickly into the water.

He stepped carefully into the middle of the tippy boat and said, "Get in, and put the light out. I can see better without it."

I stepped in and nearly turned the boat right over. Killian's paddle slammed hard against the gunwale as he caught himself. A loud hollow boom echoed across the river into the fog.

"Jeez, Alex, what *are* you, an elephant?"

"Sorry."

"Get the other paddle. Don't let it bang the side of the boat, whatever you do!"

From the stern, Killian maneuvered the canoe up the shore past Breakneck Mountain and across from where Bannerman's Island should have been, if there wasn't so much fog. At first the fog settled right down on the water. Then it lifted a few feet, and we glided under it as if under a puffy blanket.

Amazingly, the fog held the faintest hint of light, perhaps from the moon or the reflection of Newburgh's city lights to the north. I watched the ghostly fog swirl as if it were alive, a thinking creature, waiting for something to happen.

"From now on, no more talking," Killian commanded even though I hadn't said anything. He pointed the canoe into the fog, which had settled again on the flat surface of the water.

We paddled steadily out into the invisible river, my heart pumping. I wondered what we might run into. How Killian knew where we were in all that fog came from some magic knowledge held only by rivermen who travel the Hudson in all seasons, in all hours.

Killian had taught me that it was dangerous to go far from shore in a light boat. The Hudson could whip up a wild chop when you least expected it—especially in the unpredictable Highlands. I felt a slight wind coming in from the west. Killian must have felt it, too.

Just then the canoe scraped bottom.

"Dang!" Killian cursed as he pushed his paddle against the gravel to pry the canoe off the shoal. "We should have done this at high tide, not low."

But he knew as well as I did, we had no choice. The tide wouldn't come all the way in for another six hours. By then it would be light out, and we'd be walking to school.

All around his arsenal, Bannerman had built a rampart with guard turrets to make a safe harbor for tugs and barges to load and unload supplies. Over the past seventy years, the rampart had crumbled and sunk. Most of it was deep enough under water at high tide, but now the entire structure was an inch or so beneath the surface, so we had to paddle far out into the river until we got to the harbor entrance.

Then we paddled around the little island, being especially quiet when we thought we were directly under Cruger's cave. We checked every little cove for a boat.

"There's nothing here," I said, disappointed.

"Shhh. You hear that?"

"What?"

"Something big out there in the fog."

The wind was up. Killian braced his paddle flat against the waves to keep us from tipping.

"There's a ship out there. Not moving. Must be anchored. Let's have a look."

The wind was brisk now, but Killian plowed his paddle deep into the river to get us to where I also heard the thump-slosh of waves hitting something hard.

The fog lifted perhaps ten feet off the waves. Suddenly, a ship.

There it was, a craft like no other, all boxy and bulky and ghostly. Its three trapezoidal sails on three tall masts were fully set, luffing into the wind as the ship swung easily on its anchor chain, as if it had just returned from some mysterious mission. But no one was aboard. The high poop deck in the stern was deserted. I noticed the distinct ribs in those ghostly sails that made each one look like a giant dorsal fin from some monstrous sailfish.

"What the—"

"What the heck is *that?*"

Even Killian, who was never surprised by anything on the river, almost let go of his paddle, so startled was he by the floating ghost-box before us.

But I knew right away what it was. Only a few days ago, while writing a history report on the Vietnam War, I had come across a picture of a Chinese junk.

"Kill, it's a junk!"

"A Chinese junk?"

"Ever seen one on the Hudson?"

"No way. Cool." Killian was more intrigued than afraid.

"Why do you suppose its sails are up? Let's get the heck out of here, Kill."

Killian skillfully guided us around the hull. The canoe grew jittery and unstable when he tried standing up to peek over the poop deck, but it was too high to reach.

"Okay, let's go."

We paddled like crazy. As we came by the western shore of the island, the canoe dipped and rose in the waves like a cork. Faintly I saw the castle wall above us reaching high into the pressing fog. The brick face vanished into mist. Then the fog dropped suddenly and swallowed the wall.

That's when we heard it. Somewhere from inside that fog. A screech, a shriek, a scream. I cannot describe it. But it came from the other side of the island, an inhuman sound cutting through the fog that no living creature ever could make. The unearthly shriek reverberated off the fog as if in some diabolical echo chamber.

Killian instantly pointed the canoe downriver toward Cold Spring. In our escape we were a perfect paddling team, stroking fast, hard, and absolutely in unison.

Into the oncoming waves we paddled for our lives. But the cry, or whatever it was, came only once. We didn't hang around to see if it would come again.

CHAPTER 6

TREASURE-HUNTING LESSON

OUR CLASS WAS READING THE STORIES of Edgar Allan Poe when Mrs. Dobson asked if anyone believed in ghosts. A few kids kept silent. Most of the boys scoffed. They muttered, "No way, José." But Killian raised his hand.

"So, Killian Maguire, do *you* believe in ghosts?" Mrs. Dobson was a nice lady but she didn't seem to take any of us seriously.

Killian said softly, "I believe goblins live in the Hudson Highlands. I believe in legends."

The class twittered.

"Killian, have you ever *seen* a goblin?"

"Not yet, I haven't. But I intend to."

Everyone, even those who had been silent, exploded with glee. I might have laughed, too, except I couldn't get that cry in the fog out of my mind. Killian had said it was just Cruger trying to scare us. But even Killian didn't know how anyone or anything could make such a noise. He said it sounded like a panther being tortured.

After school Killian told me about the goblins that haunted the Highlands—they were written about in the journals of the earliest Dutch sailors. When the fur trader and merchant Robert Livingston and his crews sailed between Albany and New York City in the late 1600s, they never traveled through the Highlands without first praying for safe passage. The quick-rising storms, powerful currents, and buffeting winds were the work of goblins, they believed. The wind and current could bedevil a sailing ship for days around World's End. If a sailor didn't offer a prayer to the goblins, there was no telling what terrible fate might befall his ship.

"Those kids don't know anything about history. In the Highlands, history and legend are the same thing," Killian said.

Later, at the river, Killian was moody. He said, "Alex, I hate school. I hate wasting my time with kids who believe in nothing. We have to go to Livingston's estate. Soon! We have to find out what Cruger knows. Then we have to find out what Cruger is *doing*."

Killian for once looked a little frantic. "We have to find out where Kidd's ship went down. That's where we'll find doubloons."

Killian was sure that the pirate's ship had sunk in the Highlands, but it could be anywhere in this fifteen-mile stretch of river.

"We need details," he said, deadly serious. "And where do the hardcore facts lodge?"

"The library," I replied.

"Right. The Livingston library at Clermont!"

So on a hot Wednesday in June, Killian hopped the northbound passenger train in Garrison, and I met him five minutes later at the next stop in Cold Spring. Most commuters like my dad went south toward the city, so the train was empty.

Heading north, we never left sight of the Hudson. First, Storm

King Mountain was a giant rolled-up porcupine on the west shore. Breakneck Mountain in the east plummeted into the dark brown water of the Highland gorge. Then the Breakneck tunnel darkened everything right before we passed Bannerman's Island.

Killian and I pressed our faces up against the window. But there was no trace of any living thing on the island, no smoke, no scrap of plastic tarp, and no strange ship moored offshore. All we saw was that eerie, decaying castle from long ago.

I noticed how the early morning light tinted the crumbling brick a bright orange. Like an evil castle in a storybook, it almost looked on fire. The turrets had long ago toppled into the river. Even from this far away, we saw the wild vegetation—the rampant forsythia, poison ivy, and sumac—covering the walls and choking the castle to death.

I tingled just thinking about that scream we'd heard.

"Think Cruger's going to come after us?" I asked.

"Nah. He'll hardly miss one map. Didn't you see all those maps?"

Something was strange about that map. And it wasn't Cruger, either. Ever since Killian stole it, he had refused to really show it to me. He said he was studying it and I could look at it after he was done.

The island fell quickly behind us. The Highlands, which the Delaware Indians had called the Endless Hills, came to an end. The land flattened out above Beacon, and we sped north for a long time before the beginnings of another range of mountains appeared far off in the northwest.

These hazy blue ridges seemed to reach up and touch the sky. They had a much different flavor than the Highlands. They were higher and more rounded with age.

"Indians used to call them the Mountains of the Sky. Those are the Catskills, Alex," Killian said.

In Poughkeepsie, the commuter train stopped. I noticed everyone was getting off.

"Now we hop a freight," said Killian, as we jumped down onto the tracks from the platform.

"What are you talking about? You didn't say anything about hopping a freight!"

"There's no local passenger service north of Poughkeepsie, except Amtrack, which goes through here at a hundred miles an hour. Don't worry, Alex. I got a friend who knows the schedules. His dad works for the railroad. There's a freight heading north in about an hour. Then one heading back late in the afternoon."

Just as Killian predicted, the long freight train pulled into the station, slowed, and we hopped an empty boxcar. This adventure was fun but I couldn't relax. I kept thinking that any moment we'd get caught and the police would come and drag us off.

We rumbled along, the door open, our feet dangling out, just gawking at the river, so close I could almost reach out and touch it.

"Look over there. That's where we fish."

Across the bright water, the Kingston lighthouse at the end of a long jetty stood alone in the river. As we pulled north along the mile-wide Hudson, the color of the river turned muddier. The water was ruffled with weeds growing up from the shallow bottom. Here began the great Kingston flats.

"Good fishing," said Killian, and suddenly he grew sullen. I prayed he wouldn't turn moody, not today.

I asked, "You thinking 'bout your dad?"

"No." He gazed stonily at the passing river. "I never think about him."

I knew this wasn't true but, lucky for me, his mood passed. He said, "This is a school day, Alex. It's time for *treasure-hunting class*."

"Treasure-hunting class? On a freight train?"

"Yeah, let's go over the details of the story, the background, the history. Now's as good a time as any. Then we can discuss the map."

"You mean it?"

"Sure. Why wouldn't I let you look at the map? We're partners!"

Killian unfolded Cruger's map and laid it over his lap, but it was face down. He kept his fists on top so it wouldn't blow away in the wind.

"Okay," he said. "Here's a quiz: What is the connection between the merchant Robert Livingston of Albany and Captain William Kidd?"

"Aw, come on, Kill. That's easy. Livingston hired Kidd to be captain of the *Adventure* galley to go out on the high seas to steal loot from pirates."

I wasn't going to be stumped on the Livingston question a second time.

"Very good. A+. But what was the *real* connection betwen the pirate and the merchant? And what happened to their friendship?

"They met in Manhattan. Or was it England?"

Killian banged the map with his fist.

"See, that's your problem right there, Alex. Treasure hunters don't just stumble on treasures. Look at Mel Fisher. He spent years researching the *Atocha*, the sunken Spanish galleon. He went to libraries. He traveled all over the world. He dove and dove. He searched for thirty years before he found it. We can't go to Clermont without a clear idea what we're looking for!"

"So, Mr. Mel Fisher, what *was* the connection? You tell me. I don't see why we have to know this stuff. This isn't history class!"

"That's where you're wrong. Big time wrong. This, Alex, is history class with a *payoff!*"

Of course I knew he was right, but I certainly wasn't going to tell him so. Killian was lucky. He had a knack for treasure hunting partly because he loved details and history. I never liked history. I was no good at remembering anything. But Killian had a great memory. I think he knew this Kidd story even better than he knew boats. He used his superior knowledge against me, too. His history lessons were getting on my nerves.

He had told me pieces of the Kidd story over the past year. I suppose if I had had a better memory, I might have put it all together myself, but it wasn't until the freight train ride to Clermont that I got the entire legend in one sitting. And that's because he made me write it down. Right there in that boxcar, I learned the history.

All the evidence Killian had collected, he claimed, proved without a shadow of a doubt that Kidd had buried his gold on the Hudson River somewhere. "In order to find the treasure, we have to know who this man William Kidd really is. We have to climb into his brain to know who we're dealing with here," Killian lectured.

"Time to take notes." He reached under his shirt and pulled out a notepad and a pen.

"Here, take this. I want you to write down the whole story from start to finish."

"Aw, Kill, give me a break, will you?" I felt like a dumb student. "This is no place to take notes."

"Okay," he said. "We'll shut the door." Which he did, and I scribbled in the weak, bouncing light coming through the cracks of the boxcar walls.

"This isn't all legend and ghost stories, Alex. This is fact! You have to memorize the facts behind the legend."

Fact fact fact, I wanted to say, but I held my tongue.

Killian said, "There will be a final exam, too!"

"Exam? Come on, Killian. Don't be ridiculous. Let me just take one little peek at the map, will you?"

"If you pass the test, you'll be rich beyond belief."

Killian never once turned the map right side up. He talked and talked as the train rumbled slowly north. And I scrawled the best I could. It's a marvel that I wrote anything at all in that boxcar.

BACKGROUND:

In late 1600s pirates roamed the oceans. No ship was safe at sea, and New York City swarmed with buccaneers. Finally the British government decided to end piracy once & for all—a group of British politicians & businessmen got together to buy a ship called the *Adventure* galley to attack the pirates and confiscate their loot (they would keep the pirate treasure as their profit). Albany merchant Robert Livingston became a partner.

WHO WAS WILLIAM KIDD?

Born in Scotland around 1645, the son of a poor minister. Ran away from home to find adventure in the Caribbean & became a young pirate. Many years later settled down in New York City, where he met Robert Livingston. Kidd was foreman on a jury that investigated Livingston's illegal business dealings & Livingston was acquitted. Years later Livingston wanted to repay the favor—he recommended Kidd to be captain of the *Adventure* galley.

TURNING PIRATE:

September 6, 1696, the *Adventure* galley with 155 men sailed out of New York harbor headed for the Red Sea, Indian Ocean & pirate island of Madagascar. For two years Kidd looked for pirates to attack but he had terrible luck & didn't capture a single pirate ship. Finally the crew threatened to mutiny. They demanded that

Kidd turn pirate himself. He then began to attack same merchant ships he had been hired to protect. Captain Kidd became the world's most notorious pirate. Grew rich in gold & maybe silver, jewels, & fine cloth. Raided merchant & pirate vessels alike.

BURIED TREASURE:

British government began to hunt Kidd down. As he fled from capture, Kidd buried treasure in at least 40 places up & down the east coast of North America. On one of his last journeys, up the Hudson, a storm drove his ship onto some rocks. Kidd hauled his gold up a mountain in the Highlands & slit the throat of his mastiff. Then he buried the dead dog over the gold because he knew that anyone who ever came to dig up that treasure would be haunted by the ghost of the dog for the rest of his days.

CAPTURE & HANGING:

Kidd had expected to come back for his treasure. In 1699 he turned himself over to the authorities in Boston, because he believed that his connections in high places would get the piracy charges against him dropped. Instead he was immediately taken to England to stand trial & was condemned to die. The *Adventure* galley's partners used Kidd as a scapegoat for their own political protection.

Killian's voice had risen into a high-pitched chant. "In December 1701 Kidd was hanged at the mouth of the Thames River in England. But the rope around his neck broke. He was hanged a second time. Then Kidd's body was left to rot on the gallows in the great seaport, his fate a warning to other pirates. The gulls picked at his flesh. The tides washed away his bones."

He ended with these sentences: "And to this day, only a small portion of Kidd's treasure has been recovered. He never came back to dig up the treasure he buried on the banks of the Hudson River as he fled from the law!"

Killian then threw back the boxcar door. "Lesson's over."

The wide-open light of the Hudson Valley flooded the boxcar like a tidal wave. The Mountains of the Sky were directly across from us. The river was only a few feet below.

"So what about this guy Livingston?" I wanted to know. "Was he *that* bad?"

"I'm getting there. Patience, patience."

But just then the train slowed to a near stop.

Killian studied the river, then looked up and down the track, his head sticking way out.

"Come on. I think this is Tivoli."

Killian grabbed the map and said, "Jump."

Before I thought about what I was doing, I leaped feet-first onto the railroad gravel. I rolled twice before landing inches from the water. Killian actually got wet. But he was laughing, and so was I.

We got out in the nick of time, too. Just then the train gathered speed, heading north toward Albany.

CHAPTER 7

CLERMONT

As IT TURNED OUT, we had jumped too soon.

The train hadn't gotten to Tivoli yet, and now we still had a few miles to reach Clermont.

The tracks stretched far out into the river and crossed a wide bay. The sun beat hard on the brown water. Today the Hudson had no traffic. No boats, no people anywhere. Only ducks bobbed on the rolling swell. This was the kind of river day Killian loved best. Here was new territory to explore.

Killian clapped his hands, and a hundred black ducks skipped over the water, beating their wings into the air. Killian shouted, "Yiiiiip yoooooo."

Two swans glided along the far shore of the bay, the curve of their necks like snowy question marks.

Killian hopped a rail and I got on the parallel rail, and we ran as fast as we could until I fell off first. We laughed together. I felt closer to Killian than I'd ever felt. I didn't want this day to end.

"If we find the treasure, Kill, maybe I'll buy a house on the river," I said.

"Not me. I'm gonna build a big fishing boat, half cruiser, half trawler. I'll take it south past New York harbor, then out to sea. *To explore the world.*"

"Is that Clermont way up ahead?"

"Must be."

High on the east bank of the Hudson, the great estate stood majestic and haughty in the midday sun, a solitary speck in the distance. Killian took up the story again.

"Don't fool yourself. Livingston was no friend of Captain Kidd. He was a terrible man." Killian grew angry. "He stole from the Indians and gave to himself. He took what he could, and he let his friend hang. A fellow Scotsman, too!"

Killian hissed the name. "Livingssston."

"Livingston came to New York from England in 1673 and then sailed up the Hudson to Albany, 150 miles on a sloop. Albany was just a small Dutch colony then. Maybe eighty houses. The French and the Indians blasted them constantly. The Hudson Valley was a wild place in those days." Killian had begun to smile.

Livingston was a shrewd businessman, all right. Killian said he learned the Iroquois language and Dutch, too, in order to trade. He got rich on furs. Finally he bought a chunk of the Hudson shoreline so he could build himself a manor.

"Guess what the robber paid the Indians for the land? For two thousand acres of prime Hudson River real estate?"

"A million dollars?"

"Nah. Get this—Livingston paid only ten pairs of stockings, six guns, ten kettles, ten axes, twenty little scissors, one hundred fish-hooks, four rolls of tobacco, and one hundred pipes!" He spit out the list of articles in disgust.

"Sounds like a fair trade," I joked, but Killian was in no mood for humor.

"The Indians didn't even know what they were doing. You see, Alex, Indians don't believe anyone can *own* land. They were tricked. That land is worth billions today. Billions!!

"After Livingston hired Kidd to captain the *Adventure* galley, some of Livingston's men joined on as crew. That's why Kidd was sailing up the Hudson in 1699—his men were on their way home. Get it, Alex?"

"Yeah, I see. Makes sense. Or why else would Kidd be so far up the Hudson River when his ship went down in that storm, right?"

"Exactly. You're catching on. Keep it up, Alex. You'll make a great treasure hunter. Just like Mel Fisher." He grinned.

Killian went on. "There's another name you don't know yet. But you will, because this guy was the worst of all—the Earl of Bellomont. He was gonna become New York's next governor, and Livingston made friends with him in England. He was one of the partners in the *Adventure* galley scheme. Bellomont was the guy who tricked Kidd, promising him freedom if Kidd turned himself in. And of course Kidd believed him. Who wouldn't? They were *partners*, for cripe's sake!"

"Like you and me."

"Right. And you wouldn't let me down, would you, Alex?" Killian glowered at me as if he wasn't one hundred percent sure of my loyalty. He picked up a rock from the railroad bed and heaved it at the river.

"Bellomont sent *his* partner to England to be hanged!"

The director of the library was at lunch. His secretary made us wait. She kept looking at us suspiciously.

"You say you're doing a school paper on Robert Livingston?"

Kill said, "Yes, ma'am. The merchant from Albany."

"Well," she said, "you know, don't you, that Clermont was

originally built in 1730 by Robert Livingston's son, another Robert Livingston?"

"Yes, we know," said Killian, but I saw a shadow of disappointment cross his face.

"You have records here of all the Livingston family, don't you?"

"Yes, we do, but . . . usually we get professors who are a little older than you two. How old *are* you boys, anyway?"

I said, "We're sixteen."

"Sixteen going on thirteen, I'd say," laughed the secretary.

Finally, John Bates, the director, returned from lunch and made us sit another ten minutes in his office while he sorted through some papers on his desk and made phone calls. He was a tall, thin man with horn-rimmed glasses, not particularly friendly.

"So, what can I do for you boys?" His voice was filled with exasperation.

I blurted out, "Mr. Bates, we've come all the way by train from Cold Spring to do research for a term paper on Robert Livingston. Can we please use your library?"

"Well, you're a little young, aren't you? Besides, which Robert Livingston might you be researching?" He held up a sharp pencil, turning it slowly between his fingers.

"The original one," said Killian.

Bates smiled slyly. He said, "I see," and leaned forward. He began to doodle on a yellow lined pad. He spoke with eyes downcast.

"You boys wouldn't be interested by any chance in a certain pirate, would you?"

Bates stood up. Unable to restrain himself, he exploded. "Well, I warn you. There is *no* treasure at Clermont. I don't want you or any other kids digging on this land, understand me?" His eyes bore into Killian as if he knew instinctively that Killian was the digger.

Killian said, "Mr. Bates, we know the first Robert Livingston built his manor somewhere else. We promise not to dig. But our research is really and truly about Livingston's relationship to William Kidd. That's what our paper is all about."

Bates hesitated, as if he were turning something over in his mind. Maybe he was impressed by Killian's persistence.

Calmer now, he said, "Well, okay. This is, after all, a public library. You're welcome to read what you can. But I'll give you one hour, no more. Then I want you boys off the estate. We've had too many kids digging for treasure here. They sneak in at night. They make ugly holes all over the lawn. If I catch them, I'll put them in jail."

Bates led us over to the manor house, through the kitchen, past a dining room with all the place settings, silverware, and crystal goblets neatly arranged on the table. We climbed what looked like the maid's stairs. On the second floor, velvet ropes were strung across various bedrooms to keep tourists from touching the valuable antiques.

In the library, six-foot-tall file cabinets were stuffed with the letters of the Livingston family, newspaper clippings, magazine articles. Behind the cabinets were shelves of old books.

Bates handed Killian a manila envelope that contained photocopies of articles written about the first Robert Livingston.

He said curtly, "This is all we have on *your* Robert Livingston."

He pulled two pairs of white gloves from a drawer.

"Here. Put these on," he ordered. "Be careful with the pages. Some are old and *extremely* delicate." Then he gusted out of the room.

But I had the feeling that Bates was just around the corner within earshot, so I wrote on a piece of paper, "You study these. I'll look at the books on the shelves. Make notes. No talking."

Killian nodded. We went quickly to work.

Exactly one hour later, Bates was telling us it was time to

leave. He put our gloves back into the drawer and escorted us outside.

"I guess you didn't find too much about the pirate, did you?" He smiled with satisfaction and watched us walk down to the tracks.

Killian was dejected. He had expected to find something—anything! But he had not found a single scrap of evidence about where Kidd's ship might have gone down in the Highlands. Now he was sure Cruger would beat us to the gold.

Killian sat down on the tracks, his head between his hands.

"Nothing," he said. He kicked the gravel. "We got nothing."

I couldn't stop my glee.

"Well, Kill, I just happened to find something for you."

Killian looked up.

"Here's a little treasure," I said as I slipped a book out of my shirt.

"Why, Alex!!! You thief. What you got there?"

"Take a gander at *this*, Kill." And with the daredevil flourish of a true treasure hunter, I handed my friend some stolen goods.

CHAPTER 8

THE QUEDAH MERCHANT

I HAD NEVER STOLEN ANYTHING BEFORE in my life. I'd always thought that if I did steal something, a siren would go off, the police would clamp me in prison for life, or a tree would fall on me. But I felt no such fear of punishment as Killian leafed through the book I had lifted. His delight masked any feelings of guilt I might have had. Besides, I reasoned, I could always take the book back when we were done with it.

"Oh, man, Alex," Killian said with his head buried in the book. "You got the real stuff here. This is what I've been looking for!"

Captain Kidd and the War against the Pirates by Robert C. Ritchie, written in 1986, had a great section on Kidd's last days as he dodged the law. Killian silently reveled in the details of the book even as I said we had better start walking in case the return freight train didn't appear. It was already late afternoon.

Killian stumbled on the railroad ties because he wasn't paying attention to where he put his feet. He read as he walked. Finally he raised his head, looked at the river, and summarized his discoveries for me.

Both Livingston and Bellomont had written to Kidd begging

him to return to New York, he said. They claimed he would be treated well and would be safe. But Kidd knew his reception would not be a favorable one.

He had long ago given up the *Adventure* galley. Teredo worms living in tropical waters had eaten the bottom of the boat. In the days of the old ships, the wooden hulls had to be taken into fresh water and overhauled on a regular basis. Kidd had not done so, and his ship had rotted from beneath him. So when he captured a richly laden Persian treasure ship called the *Quedah Merchant*, he burned the *Adventure* galley. Kidd then sailed the pirated *Quedah* across the rough seas south of the Cape of Good Hope. He stopped at Ascension Island for fresh turtle meat. Turtles were loaded on board and placed on their backs to immobilize them— they could be eaten for months on long voyages.

In April 1699 Kidd arrived on the Caribbean island of Anguilla.

"Doubloon country," said Killian.

Kidd tried to hide in the deserted coves of the West Indian island. It was here that he discovered that the government had declared him a pirate and had ordered an all-out manhunt for him. But Kidd continued to send letters to Bellomont in New York, hoping for a pardon. His only chance would be to prove he was no pirate.

Meanwhile, hiding the *Quedah*, a 500-ton mercantile ship, proved difficult. In violation of his contract with Livingston and the other partners, Kidd continued to sell off some of the *Quedah's* treasure. He bought a small sloop, the *San Antonio*, to take him to Boston and New York.

On the pirate island of Hispañiola ("It's now Haiti and the Dominican Republic," said Killian), the *Quedah* was offloaded. Five smaller ships drew up to the massive boat to take its load of bales of East Indies cloth, muslins and calicoes, satins and silks. Then the cloth was sold.

Killian looked up again.

"So Alex, you might be right. Listen to what was aboard the *Quedah Merchant*." Killian read aloud:

It is impossible to state with accuracy just how much Kidd and his men profited from selling their cloth goods. The estimates made by others . . . range from £16,000 to £1,200 plus 2,000 pieces of eight. . . . It is certain that the sellers managed to get rid of bulky goods and acquire more portable forms of wealth. Each man who decided to continue on with Kidd moved his belongings and any goods he had onto the *Antonio*.

"It says here that Robert Livingston himself stated that Kidd had £500,000 in sterling aboard the *Antonio*."

"I told you, Kill. There *were* pieces of eight! Sterling. That's silver!"

"Yeah, I know. But Kidd would have bought gold doubloons. That's the thing to buy in the Caribbean."

Stubborn Killian went back to reading quietly to himself. He didn't care if he stumbled over the railroad ties.

On the long stretch of track across the big bay at Tivoli, thinking the freight would never come, I was throwing rocks at the river when suddenly, without warning, a floodlight rounded the bend far off in front of us. I saw it first. I wasn't scared. My head full of Kidd history, I wasn't thinking about danger.

By the time I heard the Amtrack horn blaring and the metal wheels scraping the rails in a futile attempt to brake, Killian was looking up into the face of a death machine traveling a hundred miles an hour. But he had looked too late to make his move. So I threw my whole body into him, knocking him over the track into the water.

His precious book flew up and out and was instantly scattered by the whistling engine into a hundred pieces of paper. Like confetti. Paper fluttering in the air, paper floating in the river, paper everywhere we looked.

In complete silence, we lay half in the water, half on the rocks, stunned, unable to move. My muscles quivered.

Killian scrambled up the embankment and was grabbing up pages.

"Come on, dang it, Alex! We gotta get it all. COME ON, COME ON!"

Ritchie's book had been offered to the train, to the wind, to the river, and now Killian was trying his best to reclaim it. In his arms he hoarded chunks of broken book, half-ripped pages, wet pages, muddy pages.

Slowly I climbed back onto the tracks to help. A feeling of hopelessness had come over me. I had no energy. This must be what earthquake victims feel, I thought.

Pages were strung out for more than a hundred yards on the long track across that wide bay. Killian looked as if he'd cry. Furiously, desperately, he collected papers until our slow-moving freight finally came along.

Two hours later, on the passenger train heading south from Poughkeepsie in the late twilight, Killian had reassembled two-thirds of the book into a tattered pile. Undaunted, he was reading aloud snippets of text. A real treasure hunter, I thought. I never doubted that Killian had what it took to find gold.

He said, "Kidd now sailed up the east coast of America, stopping in many places. He stopped 'here and there to let men leave the ship and to collect the latest tidings from New York.' That's what the book says, Alex."

"Really?" Killian's words seemed so far away. The immense river landscape outside our windows was dissolving quickly into night.

"Perfect!" shouted Killian. "Kidd knew he might be trapped

when he got home, so he seeded the treasure all up and down the coast! He'd come back later to dig it up. But there was no 'later' because Bellomont betrayed him!"

Killian's thinking was traveling in circles. Hadn't we just established these facts?

When we passed Bannerman's Island, I swear I saw Cruger's fire flickering. Killian put the pile of pages down on his lap. His hands were shaking. His face went pale.

He unfolded Cruger's map.

"By gosh. I found it."

"What?" I said.

He handed me the topographic map he'd taken from Cruger's cave. For the first time, he actually wanted me to see it. Then he handed me the page he had been reading.

Here was a sheet of paper that could not have come from Ritchie's book. The page looked as if someone had typed it on an old typewriter. It was smudged with dirt. Perhaps it had been inserted into the book someplace and only came free when the train split it apart.

It read: "Many people believe Kidd's ship went down in a storm on what is today called Jones Point, which is the rocky ledge that comes off Dunderberg Mountain. Years ago, local fishermen had a different name for those rocks so treacherous to sailors. More fittingly, the area went by the name of *Kidd's Point*."

I looked at the map that Killian had kept secret for days. Clusters of six black Xs were scattered over the Highlands. There was a cluster of six Xs on Bannerman's Island itself, another cluster across the river at the base of Storm King Mountain. And far to the south, below Garrison, across from the town of Peekskill, the name Dunderberg Mountain was written in black marker. Only two Xs had been marked along the strip of land that came off the mountain into the Hudson.

"So Cruger's been there already."

"Yeah," said Killian. "And he's still there! But he hasn't found the gold."

"How do you know?"

"Look here." Killian pointed at the dates written beside the Dunderberg Xs. One was marked May 15. The other was May 31, which was only a few days before we had met Cruger on the island.

"I don't get it."

"Alex, these Xs mark test pits. Cruger digs in clusters of six pits per location—then he tries another place. Two weeks ago he had only done two pits around Dunderberg. That means he has four more to do. We gotta get there first!"

"Then it's still out there."

"Yeah, but Kidd wouldn't have buried the gold right down by the water. No way. He was a seaman. He knew about the tides. I'm sure he climbed the mountain, where the trees are bigger. Remember the big tree?"

"Yeah."

A million questions swirled in my brain. Before he sailed for Boston, could Kidd really have slipped through New York harbor in the *San Antonio*, past Manhattan Island, under the cover of night, to sail up the Hudson? Did Livingston himself know that Kidd was coming to him when Kidd was caught in a storm off Kidd's Point? Had Cruger read the Ritchie book? Was the book we saw in the cave Clermont's second copy of the same book?

For each additional piece of information uncovered in the mystery of a treasure tale, five new questions emerged. It was like a puzzle that kept growing more complex as we tried to put the pieces together.

The conductor called out, "Cold Spring, Cold Spring."

It was black outside. We couldn't see the river at all.

My head swarmed with details. Wonderful details. Details that gave me hope once again.

When I said goodbye to Killian, he hardly noticed. I'm sure he was thinking about Cruger and the race to see who could get to the treasure first.

I said, "Kill, don't forget. The next stop is yours."

I don't think he heard me.

Alone on the platform, I watched the train lights pull away from the station. The dark river nearby gave me such a lonely feeling.

CHAPTER 9

FLORIDA

THE DAY BEFORE SCHOOL LET OUT, Killian told me the bad news. We sat together on the town dock. The sun was setting over Storm King Mountain.

"I'm not going," he said, kicking the water with his toes.

"Going where?"

"To Florida. Dang dang dang."

Killian looked desperately at the river.

"They bought a house. We're supposed to leave in two stupid weeks. I don't want to go to Florida. Florida's for old people."

Killian gave the water a big kick with his bare foot. He slapped the dock with the palm of his hand.

"I hate Florida."

Killian had never been to the state. What he meant was, he loved the Hudson. No place on earth could match this river.

"My father's a jerk!"

"Listen, Kill, maybe we'll get lucky. Maybe we'll find something before then."

"You bet I will. I told my dad I'm gonna camp on the river all week. Dang it! He knows I don't wanna move to *Florida*."

Killian now kicked the river so hard his foot hurt.

"Can I go camping with you?"

"You're my partner, aren't you?"

"Yeah, but I don't know if Mom and Dad'll let me do it. Where do you want to camp first? Dunderberg?"

"And Bannerman's, too."

"Bannerman's? Why there?"

"I wanna explore the castle. Maybe we'll scare Cruger like he scared us. Maybe there's more maps. We can dig around his cave. Find out what he knows!"

Killian was smiling that fanatic smile again.

"Kill, he could be dangerous. We don't know anything about the guy."

"Well, I don't give a dang! Let the old crazy just try something. Ha."

"Kill?"

"What?"

"I got a call from Clermont. Bates wants it back."

"What?"

"The book. What do you think?"

"Too dang bad," said Killian.

"But I could get into trouble."

Killian ignored me. He kept making his plans. "First Dunderberg," he said. "Then the island, then Dunderberg for the final time—to take that sucker outta there."

"Kill, don't you care if I get into trouble? I got the book for *you*, you know!"

Killian wheeled around and stared at me. His face was distorted, ugly.

"No, I don't give a dang. I'm being shipped out to Florida, and you worry about a stupid book! *Cruger's out there*, Alex. He's getting *close*. We gotta stop him. I gotta get there first!"

Killian jumped up.

"Remember, Alex. *I* told you about this treasure! I don't *need* you. I can find it alone if I want."

He turned and walked away. Over his shoulder, all he said was, "Be at my dock tomorrow at two p.m. Bring a sleeping bag, mess kit, food."

CHAPTER 10

DUNDERBERG MOUNTAIN

MY MOM AND DAD know something's fishy," I said.

"Just get in," barked Killian. "So where's your stuff?"

"They said I can't camp. They said the river's too dangerous."

"Ha! What do they know about the river! *Carpetbaggers.*" Killian shrugged. Anyone who wasn't born and raised in Cold Spring and Garrison was a carpetbagger. Killian used the term for all the newcomers moving up from the city.

"They're not carpetbaggers. Don't say that."

"They are, too. So are you."

"They're just cautious. Like any parent would be."

"So lie to 'em," he shot back. "Tell them you're going to someone's house for a week. Tell them you're hittin' the road. Tell them *anything.* I don't care. You coming or not?"

"I can come for the day if you give me a ride back by eight or nine tonight."

"Aw, jeez. What kind of namby-pamby treasure hunter are you, anyway?"

"I'll try to sneak out again tomorrow night. But they're watching me, Kill. I'll have to be careful."

"Just get in."

Killian's Alumacraft was jam-packed with gear—tent, sleeping bag, spades, shovels, mess kit, water jugs, flashlights. Killian had enough supplies to last a year in the woods.

"Got enough stuff?"

No answer.

"Where do you want me to sit?"

"Anywhere."

I finally sat on top of his tent. Killian didn't look too happy about anything.

The river was oddly misty that afternoon. I felt chilled, as if an October fog had rolled in off the Atlantic out of season. It was a strange, cold mist for June.

Killian drove the Alumacraft full-bore for Dunderberg Mountain. South of Garrison, the tide ebbed in great whirlpools that a slower boat might have had trouble negotiating. Killian's Alumacraft just danced over the turbulence like an airboat over sawgrass.

When the mist got too thick he slowed down to trolling speed. He seemed a little disoriented today. He couldn't find the western shore around Iona Island.

"I don't understand it. We should be there by now," he mumbled as we trolled slowly through the misty soup.

The motor kicked, coughed, and died. The propeller had struck a rock. Killian hadn't seen the rock coming.

He swore as he tilted up the motor. The sheer pin had severed, and the propeller whirled limply on its shaft. Without a second thought Killian took off his clothes and jumped into the river with a new sheer pin in this teeth and a pair of pliers in his hand. He replaced it right on the shaft!

I pulled him back into the boat. He didn't even say thank you.

Killian left the motor tilted up as he began to row us quietly along the shore. He was listening to the fog the way a robin listens for earthworms.

The ebb tide helped us along.

"Here it is," he said, and he jumped out to pull the boat up onto the rocks. He secured the bow line to the roots of a tree. I followed him as he moved along the bushes, stepping in the deep mud of low tide.

It wasn't twenty minutes later that we heard banging in the mist. We dove behind a boulder, then ever so cautiously moved toward the loud sound.

The first thing we saw was a bright light cutting the mist. A hurricane lantern hung low down on the mast over the poop deck of Cruger's junk.

In a small harbor on the south side of the mountain, Cruger had wedged his boxy boat into a rocky space, a natural slip. From the way he was quickly taking down his sails, I figured he must have just arrived from the island.

When the sails were furled, the treasure hunter ducked below into the tiny cabin. He emerged with a long cylinder that looked like a huge roll of wallpaper. He took it aloft into one of the three masts. From the very top he threw the roll out over the water. Immediately about a third of his junk was covered from view.

He attached the top of the long sheet of cloth to the top of the mast before he climbed down and repeated the action with an identical roll from the second mast.

When he finished climbing the third mast and shooting a roll over the rest of his boat, Killian and I knew exactly what he had done. The Chinese junk had disappeared without a trace. The color of the cloth, even in the grey mist, was the color of the mountain vegetation behind, light spring green with earthy browns mixed in.

He'd camouflaged his boat. No one passing on the river would ever be able to see it here in this little rocky nook, covered in a perfect imitation of spring flora.

Cruger now jumped ashore with a shovel and a big sack, which he began to lug up the mountain. Quickly he disappeared into the mist.

Killian said, "So that's how he does it!"

"No wonder we didn't see his boat on Bannerman's the first time."

"Cruger's a genius. Come on. We gotta set up camp."

Killian raced to the boat. I helped him take all his gear up Dunderberg to a flat area just large enough for a tent. We set up camp and waited until dark.

Killian didn't feel like talking. He wouldn't tell me his plan. With dusk the mist vanished. Stars rushed to fill the sky. Across the bay, the lights of Peekskill reflected off the water. It had turned out to be a perfect night. I was sorry I couldn't stay.

Finally, Killian said, "Okay, if you need a ride home, let's go."

I followed him to the boat. Killian was making me feel like a second-rate, cop-out treasure hunter. I wanted to punch him as hard as I could. But I didn't dare. He was so moody, he could cut me out of this treasure search at the slightest provocation. Not to mention the fact that he was big enough to flatten me in a fight.

Killian ran the motor very slowly past the junk and up Dunderberg's shore until we were well out of range from any spot Cruger could hear us. Then he gunned the motor to cross the river. About a half mile out, we suddenly came to a stop.

His arm shot out. "Look up there!"

High on the black silhouette of Dunderberg was a flickering light. It was a solitary speck of flame in an immense mountain darkness. Cruger was digging another test pit by torchlight. Killian had been right.

When we reached the Cold Spring dock, Killian's voice softened. He said, "Okay, Alex, I'll explore the Dunderberg tonight. I'll find out where Cruger's digging. Tomorrow night I'll head to Bannerman's. Cruger won't bother me. I'm gonna spend tomorrow night on his island. If you wanna join me, meet me at midnight tomorrow. Right here."

"Sure," I said. "Killian?"

"Yeah?"

"Are we still partners?"

"Yeah, but if you don't show—I'll know you're out."

"Okay, it's a deal."

Killian pulled the cord and put the motor into forward.

I called out, "Be careful, Kill."

He gave me the thumbs-up sign. Shooting across the dark river without running lights, the boat was quickly swallowed from sight.

CHAPTER 11

BANNERMAN'S AGAIN

IT WAS SATURDAY. I HAD THE WHOLE NIGHT. I told my parents I was staying at a friend's house. I didn't want to lie to them, but there was no other way to get the whole night. I had to be with Killian. At least for Bannerman's Island.

I waited at the pizza shop until eleven. Then I walked down to the dock and watched the wind toss the waves into a froth.

Killian's boat raced into Cold Spring exactly at midnight. I took this punctuality as a sign that he still liked me.

I put my knapsack into the boat and pointed my flashlight into Killian's face.

"Don't." He pushed it aside. How tired Killian looked! As if he hadn't slept in days. His eyes were bloodshot, his hair all crazy and uncombed.

"What happened to *you*?"

"Bad dream, that's all. Get in."

Killian had had his most vivid dream about Captain Kidd ever. It was, he said, the worst nightmare of his life.

What made this dream different from most nightmares was that he swore even after he was awake that he'd seen the pirate's ghost not on Dunderberg but in his tent. It seemed so real.

The dream was full of stormy weather, he said. The wind tossed the leaves into a frenzy. In the dream, Killian was searching along a small stream until he found a big tree. He huddled beneath it for protection against the storm. As he curled up for warmth, suddenly from the creek bed there rose a vapor. The vapor took shape, and the pirate himself stood in full buccaneer dress, earrings and bandanna, knives and all.

This time Killian could see a ghastly and haggard face, full of terror and anger. The ghost reached a long bony finger toward the river. The ghost's mouth was open in a scream.

The pirate was not signaling for him to come closer. He'd been wrong about this. The pirate's arm was stretched out to tell him to leave the area, immediately. Or else!

"Or else what?"

"I don't know. How should I know?" Killian's voice was weak. "The arm means something bad. But I don't care."

Killian had awakened in a sweat. At two a.m. he had climbed to where Cruger was working. He found Cruger digging by torchlight. His pit was larger than a bulldozer. Cruger was so far down in the hole, he was invisible from the nearby woods.

"Dang it all! That crazy man can work. You should've seen him, Alex. He didn't stop. He shoveled all night long. He must have pulled a hundred buckets of dirt out of that pit. I watched him work until daybreak. Then suddenly he went into his tent. Just like that. It was strange. Why does he dig only at night? I don't get it."

"Maybe he thinks we can't come out at night 'cause we're kids. Maybe that's why he's digging in the dark. To keep us away from him."

"Could be. Could be, Alex. You know, you might be right."

Tonight the water was flooding northward. The wind and the tide pushed our boat along like the giant hand of some goblin. Long rolling swells rocked the boat. The river fought the wind, making a kind of crazy up-and-down-and-all-around motion.

Spray came over the gunwales and soaked our faces. I began to feel seasick. Killian, however, was revived by the river. He yelled above the noise of the motor and the wind, "I *love* it. Ha ha. I *love* it! The Hudson *forever!*"

The engine sputtered and was about to stall, but Killian fiddled with the mixture dials and the motor revved up again. I prayed that he'd brought enough gasoline.

Killian slowed as we entered Bannerman's tricky harbor. Together we dragged the boat onto the beach directly under the walls of the ghost castle.

From the moment I put my foot on the island, I felt a wave of foreboding—something bad was about to take place.

Killian reacted to the island as if he'd been personally challenged, as if someone had dared him again to jump out of Mrs. Dobson's window.

"Come on, Alex. Let's explore," Killian blared. He ran through the ruins like a crusader. Killian showed not a trace of fear. He knew Cruger was miles away on the Dunderberg, digging by torchlight.

Our flashlights poked into the night, "NO TRESPASSING" signs were hammered into the trees and plastered onto the deteriorating brick walls.

"I wonder if there are any explosives still on the island," said Killian.

"What if we stepped on a bomb!"

"Maybe we'll step on that panther's tail."

Killian whooped. "Bring on the ghost," he shouted. His voice ricocheted off the four walls. "BRING IT ON."

"Here's where we'll camp," he said.

"Right inside the castle?"

"Where else?"

I noticed a small dufflebag tied to Killian's knapsack.

"What've you got there?"

"Equipment," said Killian.

He unzipped the bag and drew out a long climbing rope, a string of pitons and carabiners. The metal pins and oval rings looked like professional rock climbers' stuff.

"You mean you know how to climb cliffs?"

"I took some lessons."

"But you're not going to climb—*these walls?*"

"You bet I am. Someone has to be on the look-out in case Cruger decides to come back tonight. Besides, I've always wanted to climb this castle."

"But it'll crumble."

"You worry too much. Live a little, will ya!"

I started searching for small pieces of wood to start a campfire. Killian set up the tarp in case it rained.

When the fire was blazing and the shadows were flickering off the four walls around us, we went up to Cruger's cave with our flashlights.

"Just as I thought," said Killian.

There was no trace of Cruger. Everything was gone, the maps, the nets, the tackle.

"Alex," said Killian. "Look over here."

Propped against the back of the cave wall was a book. Obviously it had been placed there for someone to find.

"Hey, it's the Ritchie book! Look. A note."

"Boys," the note read, "I hope this helps. Your pal, Cruger."

Killian began to laugh. "It's a joke. Don't you see?"

"What are you talking about?"

"He wants us to go to Dunderberg because he knows the treasure's not there!"

"Not there??"

Killian was still laughing. "Listen, Alex. Cruger has probably dug most of his six test pits on the Dunderberg. He never digs more than six pits in any location, right?"

"Right."

"So he's coming up with a big nothing on the Dunderberg. He knows something's not connecting, right?"

"Right."

"So, like any good treasure hunter, he's got a new location in mind. And now he's trying to get us to make the same mistake he's been making. He *wants* us to dig on Dunderberg. Don't you see? He wants to keep us one step behind him."

"Yeah," I said, but it sure didn't make sense to me.

"Anyway," Killian said, "now you have a book to give back to Clermont."

We hiked down to the castle and got into our sleeping bags.

I was dozing when Killian suddenly leaped to his feet.

"Almost forgot!"

Killian grabbed his rope and climbing equipment and marched to the tallest wall of the castle.

"That broken turret up there will be our lookout."

"Come on, Kill, forget it. It's too dangerous."

"*Too dangerous, too dangerous*," Killian teased. "Give me a break, Alex."

Helplessly I watched him scale the feeble wall. In the firelight I saw him hammer in one metal piton. He pulled himself up. He hammered in another piton, and then put his sneaker on the piton below. Each new spike he hammered into the wall an arm's reach above him. He clipped the oval metal carabiners to the pitons and ran the safety rope through these rings as he rose higher on the wall.

I stood beneath him. If Killian fell, maybe I could break the impact.

Killian kicked away chips of brick and cement that fell into my eyes. I had to squint. My stomach grew queasy, so I looked away.

When Killian reached the top of the seven-story wall, he climbed deftly into the ruined turret.

He yelled down, "You have to see this! Come on up here!"

My legs felt like string.

"I can see all the way to the Dunderberg and Peekskill Bay. Holy mackerel!"

Black clouds raced past the stars. The distant lights of West Point were strung along the river's edge like pearls.

"Any sign of Cruger?" I shouted into the wind.

He didn't hear me.

Again I shouted, "SEE CRUGER?"

"I don't even see his *dog*, ha ha ha," Killian yelled back. Then he kicked away from the wall.

My heart ached when I saw Killian drop so fast. The firelight threw Killian's shadow against the wall as he swung back in.

I didn't notice right away that Killian was letting the rope slide around his legs and through his gloved hand. The rope made a zipping sound as Killian rappeled off the wall. He kicked again and again, each time a little farther out, and each time he looked as if he were floating in mid-air downward along the wall, like a black spider spinning himself outward on his web.

And now Killian was on the ground, laughing and running over to the fire to get warm.

"Dang, Alex, what a feeling. You *have* to try it."

"I don't feel so good. Besides . . . you know I'm scared. Why do you push me all the time?"

"Too bad," was Killian's response. "You don't know what you're missing."

"You don't have to be mean, for cripe's sake. Not everybody can be as brave as you."

Killian just walked away from me. The pitons and the rope were already in place now for the next scaling. Killian didn't linger. Skillfully he scaled the wall again. He planned to check the Highlands every hour until daybreak.

After Killian's third climb in two hours, I finally closed my eyes and fell into a deep, disturbing sleep. I dreamed about the Delaware Indians who refused to visit the island at night. I pictured them camping on the mainland shore looking distrustfully at the little island across the narrow strait. I heard them thump the ground with their feet in a dance around a fire. I heard the bats zipping through the air over the dark river. Then I heard the Indians jump and land on their feet all at once in a great earth-shaking *thump*.

But when I woke, the stars were gone. A blanket of cloud had blotted the sky. It was beginning to dawn. The fire had gone out. The powerful wind was tossing giant waves against the shore like thunder.

"Kill?" I shouted into the night.

"Killian? Where are you?"

A sound came from the base of the wall. I ran.

Killian was lying under a heap of climbing rope. How long had he been there?

"Killian! Killian! KILLIAN!"

His breathing was irregular. I know he heard me. He tried to move but he couldn't.

"Don't move," I shouted.

I had to get help right away. I covered Killian with a sleeping bag. I tied the tarp over him to keep him dry in case it started to rain. The air was damp, and the wind smelled of rain.

"I'll be back, Kill. Don't move. I'll be right back. I'll get help. You'll be okay."

Killian moaned.

I ran for the boat.

My stomach went topsy-turvy when I saw the madness of the river. Never had I seen water so wild. The waves rose and crashed against the island like ocean waves in a hurricane.

I pushed off the beach and threw myself into the Alumacraft. Water sloshed at my feet. I should have baled it out, but I didn't think there was time.

I pulled the choke and yanked the cord so desperately I almost fell in. Luckily it started on the first try.

I took it slow out of the harbor. Each wave sent the boat's bow into the air like a rocket. Thank God the tide was almost all the way in. If I hit one of the sunken ramparts around the island, I'd shear the pin and have to row to shore.

With the motor on half full, I kept out of the channel and hugged the east bank as the boat bounced like a bronco. The tide was now running out to sea against an army of waves. Nothing could be trickier for boating, especially in the semi-dark. And no one could help me. No one was on the river this early.

It began to rain. My face stung. A cold spray drove into my eyes.

I ran that boat into one big roller after another. I knew I was okay if I kept the boat straight into the cresting waves. But whenever the waves pounded from the side, I was sure the boat was doomed. The more I steered into the wind, the better the boat handled.

The big problem was that by going in the direction of the wind I was forced to head away from shore—away from Cold Spring. Finally I drew up parallel to the village lights. But still I was a long way from shore.

That's when I decided to take the waves directly onto my side. It was my only chance. Now or never.

The first dark wave hit as I turned sharply. The force of the water sent me up and around. As I came down the side of the second six-foot wave, the third wave crested over the stern and began to swamp the small boat.

Only a hundred yards from shore, the waves were just too big. Making headway was no longer possible. The boat yawed and hemmed. The wave that swamped me was the smallest wave of all, maybe a three-footer. But bigger waves had set the boat up and down and turned it around so that I'd lost control of the craft. Too much water was sloshing around at my feet, and the boat did not handle normally.

When the Alumacraft rolled, it rolled so smoothly I couldn't tell what was happening.

I hit the water hard. My mind went blank and my body froze in a liquid so cold it felt like ice. My first conscious feeling was disbelief. This could not be *me* here in the waves.

Thanks to Killian's training, I was wearing his life jacket. Killian had told me also to kick off my shoes if I ever went over. My feet were numb, but my legs moved better in the water after I dropped my sneakers.

Panic came next, when I realized the boat was gone. Gone! I was alone.

But I heard a muffled sound from somewhere just below me! Somewhere beneath the howl of the wind and the crash of the waves, an engine was giving its death rattle, still running beneath the surface, gurgling, shooting engine smoke to the surface. I couldn't breathe.

I felt a hard object against my leg. Could it be the boat?

I pushed off and swam for my life, gasping for air.

I swam toward the lights that were visible only when I crested on a wave. In the troughs of the waves I had no sense of direction. I swam with more might than I'd ever summoned before.

I would never have reached land if the wind hadn't been driving the water eastward. The waves hurled me onto the dock like a piece of litter.

A moment later, I dragged my numb body upright. I could not feel my legs. They moved automatically. I shouted and ran at the same time. I ran banging my fist into a door, any door, the first door I came to. It was the hotel at the water's edge.

I don't remember what I said. Probably I babbled. I do recall someone wrapping me in a wool blanket. I remember a big fire. I remember soft voices and hot water.

And then my dad stood there shaking his head. "Oh, Alex," he kept saying. "Why, why?" His face was wet. He looked like he'd been crying, but it might have been from the rain outside.

He hugged me for a long time.

CHAPTER 12

A GHOST BARKING

I LEARNED THE NEXT MORNING that because I had reached the hotel in less than twenty minutes, Killian would be okay. He had been rescued by the Coast Guard in a force 7 gale and taken to the hospital in Cold Spring. He'd lost some blood from internal bleeding. He had sprained his ankle. Remarkably, the doctor said, he would be up and running around in only a couple of weeks. "You're one lucky boy," the doctor told him. "Lucky you have a friend like Alex."

Frank Maguire never left his son's side until Killian was definitely out of danger. The fisherman kept a vigil like a statue above Killian's bed all through that first night.

When I stepped into the hospital room, Mr. Maguire's eyes were red with lack of sleep. But he smiled with gratitude. Killian was conscious, and everything was going to be all right.

When Killian's dad left finally, we were alone.

Killian said in a weak voice, "Thanks."

"Forget it."

"Dad found the boat. The motor's okay. Has to be cleaned, that's all."

"Did you tell your dad about the treasure?"

"Sure."

"Was he angry?"

"A little."

"Does he believe the treasure exists?"

"I don't think so."

Killian looked sad. He rapped his hospital bed with his knuckles. He said without much conviction, "Dang it all, I'm going to crack this nut if it's the last dang thing I ever do."

"I thought we were finished."

"No way. I wonder where Cruger's going to dig next."

"But you have to go to Florida, don't you?"

"Florida's off for now."

Killian had a sly look on his face.

"What?" I said.

"I SAW HIM."

"Who?"

"Cruger. Who else, dummy? I was on the wall for an hour, with binoculars. I saw him sail past Bannerman's. At first I thought he might come to the island. It was like a ghost ship, no running lights, only those big sails driving the boat with the wind, bobbing on the chop. Alex, it was strange. So eerie! It was like he was just sailing around in that gale. For fun!! He went back and forth, back and forth."

"Fun?" I said. "Some fun."

"Alex?"

"What?"

"I heard it."

"What do you mean?"

"You're not gonna believe this."

"What?"

"It might have been the wind. But I swear I heard . . . *barking*."

"Aw, come on, Kill."

"Yelping. Not like real barking. Not like a real dog."

"A fake dog?"

"I'm serious. The south wind carried it to the island. It was all jumbled up with the fury of the storm. You've never heard anything like it. That awful wind and the barking from the sky." Killian, who claimed to be scared of nothing, looked nervous. Frightened, even.

"You okay, Killian?"

"I was coming down to get you. I wanted you to hear it. It couldn't have been Cruger."

"Sure it was Cruger, Kill. It had to be."

"When I came down, I left my glove up top. My hand . . . locked. Then I had to let go. The rope burned my hand. Look!"

Killian peeled away a large gauze bandage to show the raw flesh that the rope had burned on the palm of his hand, as he fell from the castle wall.

"Wow, looks like mush."

"Listen! When you come tomorrow, bring the charts from my house. I want to check something. Okay?"

"You still want to keep looking?"

"You bet. I'm gonna crack this nut." He didn't even try to smile.

Killian's eyes had regained only a fraction of their fanatic stare. And he seemed full of despair. As if he knew in his heart that finding the treasure was a hopeless cause.

CHAPTER 13

THE FINAL CLUE

At home Dad put his arm around Mom's shoulder and said, "Okay, Alex. Your mom and I want to know what's really going on."

There was no hiding it anymore. I confessed everything. About why a man named Bates had left angry messages on the answering machine. About the treasure, about Killian's belief in gold doubloons.

"I was only doing it for you, Dad. To help the family."

Dad seemed more concerned about my stealing the book than he did about the treasure hunt.

"You know how we feel about stealing," he said sternly. But he reached over and hugged me.

"Alex, thanks for wanting to help. But you don't have to find a treasure for me. I've got money. Maybe it's not as much as I'd like to have. No one has as much as they really want. But it's plenty for you, me, and Mom."

"It's true," Mom agreed. "We have just enough. The Hudson's

too dangerous, Alex. You shouldn't be messing around out there. I don't want you out there. Please."

"It's not so dangerous, Mom. Killian knows what he's doing."

"Then why is he in the hospital?" Mom looked worried.

"Killian grew up here, Alex. You didn't." Dad was angry again.

"But, Dad—"

"Your mom's right. We all love treasure stories. Captain Kidd might have left a pirate chest around here. Who knows? And maybe someday it'll be found. But I want to know how you intend to repay the Clermont librarian for taking that book."

"I'll work this summer."

"You bet you will. No treasure is worth stealing something that doesn't belong to you. Understand?"

"Yes."

"I don't *need* a treasure. My treasure is my family. Do you understand that? I'd rather have you safe than all the gold in the world."

"Yes, Dad."

"You're not going to like this, Alex. As punishment, your mom and I have decided we want you off the river. No more playing around out there. From now on, you're grounded."

Mom looked so anxious that I wanted to reach up and kiss her to take away her worries.

"Understand?"

"Yes, Dad."

I got off easy, really. For the next few days I wandered around the village in the afternoon, killing time after my long morning visits with Killian.

Right across the street from the hospital I discovered the Putnam County Historical Society Foundry School Museum. A tiny building, this "museum" was more like someone's old house. When I walked in, the room smelled moldy.

From behind a desk stacked high with books, an old lady with white hair stood up. I guessed she was the curator. Her cane reached out and touched me on the shoulder.

She said, "And what do *you* want, young fellow?"

"I'm just looking."

"Looking for something in particular?"

"You got any books about local legends?"

"Local legends, eh?" She tapped her way back to the desk. "Mmm. Our local paper, the *Cold Spring Recorder*, goes all the way back two hundred years. There's local history in there. Is that what you want? Something like that?"

"I guess."

"You guess. But you don't know?"

The old lady shook her head as if to say "crazy boy." She pointed her cane to a corner of the room stacked to the ceiling with newspapers.

I didn't think I'd find anything when I ran my hands through the time-yellowed pages of one issue after another. But it wasn't ten minutes later that my eyes caught the name *Kidd*. My heart skidded to a stop.

Here, buried in the museum stacks in a little Hudson River town, was a June 10, 1880, issue of the *Cold Spring Recorder*, in which the editor had focused his weekly column on the local legends of one Captain William Kidd.

I read quickly. I nearly tore the old pages.

More than a hundred years ago, it seems, pirate legends were common in the area. The editor claimed that everything seemed to revolve around Indian Brook, a small stream running into the Hudson River between the villages of Cold Spring and Garrison.

I called out to the old lady, "Is Indian Brook still there?"

"What do you mean *still there*? Of course it's still there. Where do you think it went? Humph."

I read on: "Tom Williams, a local farmer, became rich over night; some think he's found Kidd's gold."

Many years ago, the editor wrote, a man named Mr. Philip Vantwist dug at the mouth of Indian Brook and is said to have struck something with his shovel. Just as he heard the sound of metal against metal, "a vessel with big white sails dashed like a phantom, noiselessly across the smooth waters of the Hudson striking its proud bow at his very feet." Vantwist swore the man standing in the bow of the phantom ship was none other than Captain Kidd himself. Vantwist turned to run, but later forgot where he'd been digging. When he and some friends returned to the brook, they found no signs of his excavations.

I had to show this to Killian right away. I begged the old lady for a pencil and a sheet of paper. Here's what I copied from the newspaper column:

COLD SPRING RECORDER
June 10, 1880

Kidd's dog has recently been spotted on the brook just below Indian Brook Falls—and not by one person alone, but by several local residents. The dog's haunts are around the bridge that spans the chasm, just below the falls sometimes being seen on one side of the bridge, sometimes on the other.

A carriage load was returning to Garrison one evening about ten o'clock with six persons in it and just as they were approaching the spot where the mighty mastiff strides, one of the company jokingly remarked, "Now let us look for the dog."

No sooner were these words uttered when suddenly a giant dog appeared alongside the cart, its bristles upright. Pulling a revolver from his pocket, the driver fired six bullets into its hide, but the mastiff was unfazed.

Each person later described a different dog, varying in color and size. The driver claimed it was fawn colored and about eight feet tall. Some said it was smaller and grayer.

Another encounter on Indian Brook has been described by Harry Startwell who lives nearby. All village residents will verify that old Harry's stories are completely to be trusted!! Well, he claims that on his way to Cold Spring one day while crossing the bridge he actually saw the dog. He whipped his horses to go faster. But of course when he looked back from whence he had come, the dog had mysteriously vanished.

I tore across the street to show Killian. But he was sleeping. The nurses told me to come back later.

I rode my bicycle down to Garrison Landing. No one was home at the Maguires'. The door was unlocked. I found the river charts in Killian's room. I spread the charts on his bed. Yes, yes, yes, here was Indian Brook, about nine miles north of Jones Point! The little stream was only a thin blue line winding its way down from the surrounding hills into the Hudson.

Then it just struck me. I had a brilliant idea. I needed to tell Killian right away. I'd wake him up if I had to.

I stuffed the charts into my pocket and raced back to the hospital. When I got to his room, Killian was awake. He was in his street clothes for the first time in days. They were letting him go home.

I began to dance around him. He was on crutches. I grabbed a crutch.

"Quit it!" he snapped.

I whooped like a cowboy.

"Killian, oh, Kill-i-an, I found a goblin story you're gonna like."

"Get outta here," said Killian, annoyed.

I threw the paper on his bed. "Read this!"

And he did. He read the article three times, about the local legends, about Vantwist, and, most important, about Indian Brook and the ghost of the dog.

"So," I said. "Kidd must have moved his treasure off the

Dunderberg the day after the storm. It's not even on the Dunderberg. It's on Indian Brook!"

The second that Killian heard my idea, he was positive it was true. He spread the charts on his bed to study them.

After a long pause, Killian said, "William Kidd was a genius! He knew they'd come looking where his ship sank, so he moved the gold upriver from the shipwreck. Here, look at this . . ."

Killian showed me on the river charts that, from a seaman's point of view, there was no other spot to which Kidd could have taken the gold except Indian Brook. At the mouth of the brook, where it flows into the Hudson, there was a great and mysterious swamp.

"Today it's called Constitution Marsh. In Kidd's day, it probably had no name. A perfect hiding place."

Rather than drag his treasure up the mountain, as we had assumed, the desperate pirate had waited until the river grew calm the day after the storm. Now both of us could picture Kidd rowing his loot in a small skiff upriver to the marsh and then to the brook. That's where the ghost of Kidd's dog was sighted. That's where Kidd cut the throat of his dog so the ghost would guard it forever.

Killian's smile made me ecstatic. Just when I thought all hope had been dashed, we were equal partners once again.

"What a pirate! What a perfect place for a treasure! *You did it!*"

Now Killian was pounding my arm until it hurt.

"Ha," said Killian. "Cruger doesn't know any of this!"

"Yeah, he's in the dark."

"We're one up on him. Just wait, Alex. You'll see. *I'm gonna crack this nut.*" Killian whooped.

I grabbed one of Killian's crutches and hobbled around the room pretending to be Long John Silver, the pirate from Robert Louis Stevenson's *Treasure Island*. Both of us hobbled around the room in a kind of buccaneer dance, roaring "Hearty har har, matey," and laughing so hard our mouths grew tired.

Then Killian said, "We'll dig at the mouth of Indian Brook, where Vantwist struck something in the soil."

Phantom ships, ghosts of dogs, ghosts of pirates. With this new piece of information I was a believer. And I wasn't thinking about what my mom and dad said, either.

Killian chanted, "I hope we see the dog, see the dog, see the dog."

"Yeah," I said. "And no Cruger!"

"Oh, him? He'll be floating around. I'll bet he's gonna keep an eye on us, all right."

CHAPTER 14

A PLAN

MEANWHILE THE BACK-BREAKING, arm-twisting, spooky work of treasure hunting had just begun. We had to confirm our hypothesis by digging up a large piece of earth. Could we find a tree that was nearly four hundred years old? Would we dig in the right spot? Without a treasure map, nothing would be certain.

Preparations would take at least a week, and we couldn't start until Killian could walk better. So we aimed for July Fourth. The whole town would be at the river's edge for fireworks. We could slip off and do our work with no one to bother us. Even Cruger, if he was around, would be distracted by the festivities.

Killian and I had a lot of time to speculate. During these idle days, Killian's leg grew stronger. He and I no longer openly disagreed about the contents of the treasure. It didn't matter to me whether it was gold doubloons or silk from Persia or emeralds or rubies or sterling. What had begun to matter to me now was what we planned to do with the treasure when we found it.

I returned the second copy of the Clermont book to Bates. I promised to pay off the other book with my summer job.

Sitting on the town dock, I said, "Kill, when we pull the treasure up, I think we should give it to the Museum of Natural History in New York."

"*Give*? What are you, crazy? After all the work we've done?"

"Okay, sell it, then."

"To a dang museum? You gotta be kidding. What are *they* gonna do with it? They'll just put it in a cellar, where it'll sit for centuries."

"But it's part of our history, as Americans."

"No way, Alex. I'm gonna sell it to the highest bidder."

Killian jumped up and tested his ankle.

"Okay, okay, come on, Kill. Sit down. We have to make plans. Don't run off on me. Not when we're this close. Please."

"We'll figure out later what we're gonna do with it."

"It's a deal."

Killian sat down again. He said, "First thing is, we have to dig without Cruger seeing us. He's out there. I know it. Every night that weirdo is wandering the river. Just waiting for us to make a move. Holiday or no holiday, we gotta be extra careful."

"Let's meet when the fireworks begin."

"Indian Brook runs down through boulders and forests halfway between Cold Spring and Garrison. How about we meet at eight o'clock at the marsh?"

"Okay. Eight o'clock."

"Don't forget your shovel."

We locked hands. Our eyes met. Something strange and distant and even a little bit cruel in Killian's eyes sent a chill into me.

CHAPTER 15

INDIAN BROOK

ALL DAY ON JULY FOURTH the river was becalmed. The Highlands were still. No wind rose off the water. A heat haze had stalled over the mountains. The river was like brown glass.

When I got to the marsh at dusk, Killian wasn't there. The mosquitoes were horrendous. I sat by the water's edge and waited for my friend. The great marsh hid the river from sight. It was indeed a perfect hiding place. I could hardly believe the dense tangle of vegetation. It was a maze of narrow channels running through seven-foot high reeds and cattails. Birds sang sleepily in the heat. I was thirsty. I drank the water from my canteen. A great blue heron stood on one leg, its long bill poised to capture an unsuspecting fish. The tide was dropping fast. Muddy ooze showed everywhere as the water receded.

Darkness fell heavily. Bullfrogs croaked. Yet for all the natural noises of the marsh, I felt an evil silence pounding my eardrums—as if some giant had placed a monstrous bell jar over the entire marsh, cutting off the air supply, making it hard to breathe.

It was pitch black when the fireworks shattered the hot spell of the marsh. Colored streaks cracked above the river. Explosions echoed off the mountain walls of Storm King and Crow's Nest. Artificial comets zipped and zoomed and fell into a hundred balls of colored fire.

At ten Killian still had not showed. I had bug bites all over me. I could have strangled him.

After one big finale, the fireworks died. The silence of the great marsh filled with frogs and crickets.

Still no Killian. I began to worry that something had happened to him. I hiked back into town. I didn't find him. I called his house. No answer.

Maybe I went to the wrong place in the marsh, I thought, so I returned to the mouth of Indian Brook. Still no Killian. The mosquitoes were worse, the heat more oppressive than ever.

I sat on the stump of a tree, with an empty feeling. Suddenly I heard a far-away scraping sound. It seemed to be coming from up the stream somewhere, so I took my flashlight and my shovel and followed the brook up into the hills. I climbed over boulders the size of cars. Over downed trees in the stream bed.

I stopped, listened. The scraping sound was still far off. The stream bed grew steep, the surrounding forest thick. Slippery logs, uprooted trees, and a tangle of branches made it very hard going.

Far above I heard cars. A long, iron bridge spanned the wide chasm. A little farther upstream I came across a waterfall. This had to be Indian Brook Falls, where the locals had spotted the dog more than a hundred years ago.

The falls were loud and cool. I couldn't hear that scraping sound. I climbed above the falls, then heard the scrape scrape again. Loud now. I put out my light. Maybe it was Cruger. I sneaked through the darkness until I saw a glimmer ahead.

I crept ever so slowly toward the light, hoping to God it wasn't Cruger.

There, underneath the biggest tree I'd ever seen, was Killian, his legs already hidden in the pit he was digging. His shovel worked fast.

I ran toward him.

"Kill, where've you been?"

Killian dropped to his knees.

"Jeez, Alex, you scared me. Don't ever do that again! Where have *you* been?"

"But you said the *mouth* of the brook."

"No, I didn't. I said the falls."

"But you never told me about the falls. How could I know where you were?"

Killian was lying to me.

"Come on!" he yelled and began to dig again. "This has to be the tree."

There was absolutely no question that *this* was Kidd's tree. It was not an oak, but a massive cottonwood with an eight-foot diameter. It had to be at least four hundred years old, maybe five hundred. Surely it was the biggest tree in the Hudson Valley.

I wondered how Killian had found it. What other things wasn't he telling me?

I jumped into the pit and began to dig alongside a person I no longer trusted. But I had never felt this close to a treasure before, and the excitement drove me to near madness. I shoveled dirt for hours without stopping.

Three-quarters of a moon rose over Crow's Nest across the river, big and bright. Not a cloud had formed in the India ink of the sky. The moon was so bright it penetrated the forest canopy along the brook. Logs and boulders were dappled in the silver through the trees.

I stopped digging.

"Wait a minute. Why aren't we digging on the other side of the tree?"

Killian, out of breath, snorted, "Shut up and dig."

"What makes you so sure?"

Killian threw his shovel into the dirt a few inches from my feet. In the moonlight he looked dangerous.

"Because this side looks exactly like it does in my dream. That's why!"

I took off my shirt and started to dig even harder. But I kept wondering, how can you trust a dream? A dream is not like a map, is it?

At first the digging was easy. The soil was soft humus. But when we came to a layer of shale, we needed the iron bar Killian had brought to break up the plates of rock.

Getting the rock up the five-, six-, and now eight-foot sides of the deepening pit was hardly easy. But we worked well as a team, passing the buckets of dirt and rock up and out of the hole. We worked way past midnight. I knew my parents would be waiting up for me when I got home. We hacked our shovels through roots as thick as ships' hawsers. My arms ached.

Meanwhile the hole deepened, and the moonlight could not penetrate to the bottom of the pit. Killian set up a flashlight to shine where we were working, but it fell into the pit. So we worked mostly in the dark.

We were maniac diggers. We now took turns in the pit. We dug for so many hours we lost all track of time.

It was the dead of night, when Killian's shovel hit something other than rock. *Chink. Chink chink chink.*

At first neither of us understood.

Unlike hitting a root, his shovel made that infamous chink sound, exactly as Killian and I had imagined so many times— the same sound Philip Vantwist had reported a hundred years ago.

Killian pushed me aside. He threw the full weight of his body into his shovel at the center of the pit. Chink chink chink.

"Try your shovel around the edges," I yelled, but he didn't hear me. He kept banging his shovel into the object like someone hysterically trying to escape a prison cell.

"No, no," I yelled.

I grabbed him. I shouted into his face. "Listen to me. Listen to me, Kill." He let me shake him. He was quivering.

"We have to widen the pit from the top. Widen it. I SAID, WIDEN IT. Otherwise we'll *never* get it out."

Killian began to work from the top. Together we broke down the sides of the pit. Finally, out of frustration, he threw his shovel away and leaped into the pit again. With his bare hands he scooped the earth, an insane archaeologist in fast motion.

Hefting the dirt in buckets seemed like a cruel job when we were so close, but I knew we had to get the dirt out. We could feel the chest with our hands. But still it would not budge.

A wind rose from the river. The breeze smelled of jasmine.

We were both so tired that we had to take a rest. When we stood on the edge of the pit, we were high enough above the river to see over the marsh. A strip of moonlight lay on the water. I could see the waves were getting bigger with the rising wind.

Killian raved, "Another storm's coming. Out of the south, too. We have to work fast. Do you smell the flowers? Can you smell them?"

"Tropical flowers."

"Oh my God. Will you look at that!" Killian pointed at the river.

There, in a thin strip of moonlit river, Cruger's junk passed like the fleeting glimpse of a ghost ship.

I turned off the flashlight. The wind danced in the branches of the old cottonwood.

Killian stared and stared at the river.

"What's he doing?" I cried. Cruger had sailed again in the opposite direction across the river through the waves.

"What's he up to, Kill?"

No answer.

"Kill, let's finish up fast."

Killian dove into the hole. I was right behind him.

We gasped for air in the swirling dust at the bottom of the pit. We worked like madmen prying and scooping the remaining earth away from the chest. I ran my hands around its rough sides, flaky with rust and studded with nails.

The chest was almost free from the dirt when Killian started to laugh. I got shivers hearing him. He laughed triumphantly as he tugged on the lid, but the lid was nailed shut.

He hollered defiantly into the wind, "*I cracked the nut, Cruger. You hear me? I* cracked the nut! Ha ha ha ha ha."

The moon had moved across the sky and now the chest lay in a beam of moonlight. I stared at it for a long time, but I did not want to open it. Not yet anyway.

This moment was exactly what we had imagined.

We're kneeling in the bottom of the pit. I lift the metal lid of the chest with two hands while you prop it open with a branch or something. Together we reach inside the ancient darkness, into Captain Kidd's secret . . .and . . .

Killian shouted, "It's now or never! Come on! Let's open it."

I hesitated. "Sure you want to?"

"Come on. What you waiting for! Give me a hand—Aw, you're useless. The heck with you!"

"Wait. What are you doing?"

Before I knew what was happening, Killian had shouldered the chest and was climbing out of the pit.

"You coming or not?"

"Yes . . . but . . . wait . . ."

I pawed at the side of the deep hole. I tried to grab onto a big rock but lost my balance.

The last I heard was a far-off shout. "Come on, Alex. I'll be at the river . . ."

My head hit something as I fell backward.

How long I lay there in the dirt I'll never know. For a long time I could not move.

Slowly I grew conscious. A terrible dankness had seeped up the brook from the marsh. The moonlight dimmed. Moonshadows grew so faint that the big tree seemed lost in the night.

I don't know how or when I first became aware of the presence. In the tree above me, in the pit below, all around, I felt a bone-chilling dankness even before I saw the apparition.

In the leaves of the great tree, as I lay paralyzed looking up out of the hole, a shimmering figure hovered. I swear as long as I live I'll never see anything like it again. A circling aura gathered in the branches. This was no fog, no thickening of mist. No.

Something there was *alive*.

A strangely condensed sort of half-light drove terror into me.

The thing seemed centered along a central spine. Dog or human, I'm not sure. But I thought I saw a face. Perhaps it was merely where a face *might have been*.

How could this be a ghost? There were no specific features, only suggestions of limbs, moving—always moving—as if in anger, restless. Like the spirit of a caged tiger.

And that was the most frightening aspect—not knowing exactly what angry thing hovered in those ancient leaves.

Then the figure vanished. There was no barking, no pointing finger, no buccaneer with knives in his belt. No dog.

And still I could not move from the floor of that dusty pit. But I saw in the brightening moonlight the silhouette of a man's body. Not a ghost. The man was peering down over the rim of the hole.

The wild hair told me who it was.

"In a little trouble, boy?" said Cruger. "Your partner did you in, eh?"

"No, he didn't," I said, even as I feared that Killian *had* done me in, just as Cruger said.

Cruger tied a rope around the tree. Then he backed himself down the rope into the pit. He was very strong. He threw me over his shoulder in a fireman's carry and pulled me out in a flash.

The wild wind tossed his hair. He looked almost handsome in the moonlight.

"So where's the fisherman's son gone with the loot, boy?"

Then, as if he suddenly figured out the answer to his own question, he sprang for the river. Loping like an animal, he crashed down the brook.

Ten minutes later, I heard the faint buzz of Killian's boat in the gusting wind. The Alumacraft raced across the wild river, a streak of silver batting the waves, escaping the madman. I knew that Killian might never stop. I pictured his boat driving down the entire length of the Hudson, past New York harbor and out to sea, to meet the world and beyond.

I held my head tight. It throbbed with pain as I started carefully down the brook. I was glad not to be in Killian's boat. It would go much faster with only one kid in it. Besides, I knew I didn't belong there next to him. Killian was special—he was so different from me. I was a minor treasure hunter compared to him. Maybe I wasn't a treasure hunter at all.

But I still hoped Killian would contact me later.

Resting on a boulder, I caught another glimpse of the river. And there under the moonlight I spotted Cruger's ghostly sails dragging his junk through the waves in vain pursuit.

Then all I heard was the wind and the leaves rustling, and I headed home.

CHAPTER 16

THE TREASURE

I DID NOT HEAR FROM KILLIAN FOR A LONG TIME. It was a if he had dropped off the face of the planet. As if there had been no Killian, and no treasure. The summer went by, and I made a couple of new friends, kids who were mowing lawns and weeding gardens for a few bucks, just like I was. School started again, and nobody even mentioned Killian Maguire. But in the fall, when the Highlands turned bronze in preparation for winter, I received this letter from Sarasota, Florida.

Dear Alex,

Yes, I'm alive and well in Florida, which is not the same as the Hudson. But it's okay here. We have a million islands to explore. They say treasure ships lie sunken on the coral reefs, so I'm taking scuba diving lessons. Dad and I go fishing for grouper, snapper, and crab. I'm sorry I didn't tell you I was leaving so soon. Sorry for not coming back for you. But I didn't have a choice. When I saw Cruger's boat, I had to clear out, go underground. I know you understand. That crazy guy will never quit. But I beat him. I cracked the nut.

By the way, my dad told me he knew Cruger back in the old fishing days. Can you believe it? Dad says he was one of the best Hudson shad men on the river. But then he dropped out. Went overseas, Dad thinks, maybe Viet Nam. Dad didn't even know he was alive still. I wonder where Cruger is now. Have you seen him? Have you been back to the island?

You were right about what was in the box. Kidd buried lots of cloth—muslins, calicoes, and silks. They're in such rotten condition, I can't send them. I can't even pick them up without everything turning to dust. But it's definitely the treasure of the *Quedah Merchant*. And here's the good part!! I found three silver pieces of eight, chunks of pounded silver with royal stamps on them. I'm sending them to you by certified mail.

And, Alex, that old chest held only one piece of gold! One doubloon!!! The most beautiful, wonderful, solid thing I've ever held in my hand. I'll never sell it to *anyone*, or give it to *any* museum. I wear it day and night around my neck, in memory of our treasure-hunting days. You've gotta see it!!!

If you want to take the silver to a museum, it's your choice. The cloth would be pretty worthless today, but it must have been as valuable as gold to Livingston and his crowd. I'm sure Kidd was heading upriver to buy his freedom—not with gold, as I had thought, but with fine Persian cloth—when the storm hit and he had to bury his loot. The rest is history. My only wish is that I could have been a better friend. I'm sure more doubloons lie somewhere in the Highlands, a pirate's haven. It's the kind of place where history and legend blend. But who knows? Maybe someday I'll come back and search again. But for now, Florida is closer to the Caribbean, and you know what that is! *Doubloon country.*

> Goodbye, Alex. We'll meet again, I'm sure.
> Your partner,
> Killian

Except for the three silver pieces of eight that arrived in the mail a few days later, that was the last I heard from Killian. But I think of him often. Some days when the Hudson is calm, I go down to the Cold Spring dock. I look out at the great river, and I long for adventure.

Often at twilight, when the waves lap at the shore and the light fades from Storm King and Breakneck Mountain, I imagine Killian returning in secret to dig somewhere in the Highlands. I picture a solitary figure, older, his hair wild, his clothes torn. I can almost see his face, completely changed since those days of our friendship. No longer youthful or innocent, but wrinkled now from too much sun. I see him standing alone in a pit, his face smudged with dirt, a shovel in his hand, his eyes crazed with an undying fever for doubloons.

About the Author

Peter Lourie has traveled widely. He has studied ancient bones with the Leakeys in Kenya, excavated a Roman archaeological site in Spain, researched colobus monkeys in the Usembara Mountains on the coast of Tanzania, and ventured into the misty Llanganati Mountains of Ecuador in search of Incan treasure. His books include *Lost Treasure of the Inca, Rio Grande, Amazon, Hudson River, Yukon River,* and *Erie Canal.* His book *Everglades: Buffalo Tiger and the River of Grass* received the ECO Award for Excellence from the Natural Resources Defense Council, and was named a NCSS-CBC Notable Trade Book and a John Burroughs Outstanding Nature Book for Young Readers. Peter Lourie lives with his family in Middlebury, Vermont.